The Beautif

D0713147

D0756533

The Beautiful Summer

CESARE PAVESE

With an introduction by Elizabeth Strout

PENGUIN BOOKS

PENGUIN BOOKS

UK | USA | Canada | Ireland | Australia
India | New Zealand | South Africa

Penguin Books is part of the Penguin Random House group of companies
whose addresses can be found at global.penguinrandomhouse.com.

Translated from the Italian *La bella estate* © 1949, 1961, 1971, 1998, 2013, 2015
Giulio Einaudi editore s.p.a., Torino
First published in Great Britain by Peter Owen 1955
Published with a new introduction in Penguin Books 2018
003

English language translation copyright © Peter Owen, 1955
Introduction copyright © Elizabeth Strout, 2018

Set in 11/13 pt Bembo Book MT Std
Typeset by Jouve (UK), Milton Keynes

Printed and bound in Great Britain by Clays Ltd, Elcograf S.p.A.

A CIP catalogue record for this book is available from the British Library

ISBN: 978-0-241-98339-3

www.greenpenguin.co.uk

Penguin Random House is committed to a
sustainable future for our business, our readers
and our planet. This book is made from Forest
Stewardship Council® certified paper.

Introduction

Cesare Pavese was born in 1908 in a rural part of northern Italy called Santo Stefano Belbo. His family returned from this home to Turin every autumn, and all his life Pavese would be torn between country and city life.

He began his writing career as a poet, eventually publishing his collection *Work Wearies* in 1936 (also known as *Hard Work*). But Pavese had always been interested in translating, and in particular, he developed a passion for the American literary voice. His first book of translation was Sinclair Lewis's *Mrs. Wreyn* in 1931, and he went on to translate many more American writers, including *Moby Dick*, and also the work of Sherwood Anderson and John Dos Passos. His belief was that Americans were writing in a new language, using the vernacular of their lives, 'a new texture of English . . . a style no longer *dialect* but *language*, reworked in the mind, recreated,' and that the contemporary Italian language of that time, he felt, was stuck in an expression that no longer could make space for all that was happening in its country.

What was happening in the country was, most notably, fascism. Pavese lived during the rise of Mussolini, and all his work is, in some way, informed by this. In 1935 he was arrested for having letters of an anti-fascist friend, and he spent a year isolated in confinement in Brancaleone Calabro, in southern Italy. Later, during the war, he was excused from going into the armed services because of asthma. But it is important to think of Pavese – to think of any writer – writing during his time and place in history, and Pavese's time was during the rise of fascism and his place was, of course, Italy, both rural and city.

Before his arrest he had become a major part of the Einaudi publishing house, which opened in 1933. He had first collaborated with its director, Giulio Einaudi, both as a creator of, and a contributer to, the magazine *La Cultura*, and Einaudi welcomed Pavese as a member of its house in 1937. They would remain his publisher and lifelong supporters, and he would work there as an editor and then editorial director for the rest of his life.

During the spring of 1940 Pavese wrote *The Beautiful Summer*, the book you have in your hand, leaving it in manuscript form until he had completed two more short novels, *The Devil in the Hills* and *Among Women Only*. These he published together under the title of *The Beautiful Summer* in 1949. In June of 1950 he received the most prestigious prize in Italy, the Strega, for this book. In August, two months later, he died by suicide, taking an overdose of sleeping pills in a rented hotel room.

About *The Beautiful Summer*, Pavese wrote in a letter to his former teacher that it was 'the story of a virginity that defends itself.' The narrative of this book is an astonishing display of a dense, almost frenzied writing – there are whispers here of the future work of Elena Ferrante – and yet the style holds always a gentle graciousness as well. This combination makes it an inimitable read; it has a style entirely its own. The story is essentially that of a young woman's fall from innocence, and while one might rightly say this story is as old as all storytelling, the manner in which this book is written makes it a completely different version of such a theme. It takes place in Turin, during a time when the city had a bohemian artistic community, and it is this community which Pavese uncovers for us.

The novel tells of Ginia, a young shop girl living with her brother, who falls in love with a painter over the course of a summer of freedom. There are three other women protagonists, although Ginia takes center stage. But the woman who leads her into these artists' quarters is an older woman, Amelia, who is experienced in the ways of the world. The dichotomy of these two women sets up a splendid device in the construction of the book: Ginia's innocence and Amelia's experience. Throughout this narrative, the reader is taken through the most deeply believable aspects of Ginia's loss of innocence. There is a generosity towards her that we see and we believe: Pavese is just stating the facts, and yet the facts are presented with an underlying charitableness to Ginia.

In his real life, Pavese had trouble with women; he felt the betrayal of them deeply. In this book, he uses those feelings and gives us the portrait of an innocent, on the verge of discovering the cruelties of love.

Elizabeth Strout

One

Life was a perpetual holiday in those days. We had only to leave the house and step across the street and we became quite mad. Everything was so wonderful, especially at night when on our way back, dead tired, we still longed for something to happen, for a fire to break out, for a baby to be born in the house or at least for a sudden coming of dawn that would bring all the people out into the streets, and we might walk on and on as far as the meadows and beyond the hills. 'You are young and healthy', they said, 'Just girls without a care in the world, why should you have!' Yet there was one of them, Tina it was, who had come out of hospital lame and did not get enough to eat at home. But even she could laugh at nothing, and one afternoon, as she limped along behind the others, she had stopped and begun to cry simply because going to sleep seemed silly and robbed you of time when you might be enjoying yourself.

Whenever Ginia was taken by a fit of that kind she would unobtrusively see one or other of her girl friends home and chatter on and on until she had nothing more left to say. So when they came to say goodbye, they had really been alone for some time and Ginia would go back home quite calmed down without missing her companion too badly. Saturday evenings were of course particularly wonderful when they went dancing and next morning she could lie in. But it did not take that to satisfy her and some mornings Ginia would leave the house on her way to work just enjoying the walk. The other girls would say, 'If I get back late, I find I'm sleepy next day', or 'If I get back late, they give me a beating'. But Ginia was never tired and her brother who was a night-worker, slept in the day-time and only saw her at supper. In the middle of the day – Severino turned over in bed when she came in – Ginia laid the table. She was always desperately hungry and chewed slowly, at the same time listening to all the household noises. As is usually the case in empty lodgings, there was no sense of urgency, and Ginia had time to wash up the dishes that waited for her in the sink, do a bit of tidying round, then lie down on the sofa under the window and let herself drowse off to the tick of the alarm-clock in the next room. Sometimes she would close the shutters so as to darken the room and feel more cut off. At three o'clock Rosa would go downstairs, pausing to scratch gently at her door so as not to disturb Severino until Ginia let her know she was awake. Then they would set off together, parting company at the tram.

The only things Ginia and Rosa had in common were that short stretch of street and the star of small pearls in their hair. But once when they were walking past a shop-window Rosa said, 'We look like sisters', and Ginia saw that the star looked cheap and realized that she ought to wear a hat if she didn't want to be taken for a factory-girl; especially as Rosa who was still under her parents' thumb wouldn't be able to afford one for heaven knows how long.

On her way down to call her, Rosa came in unless it was getting too late, and Ginia let her help her tidy round, laughing silently at Severino who, like all men, had no idea what house-keeping involved. Rosa referred to him as 'Your husband', to keep up the joke, but quite often Ginia's face would darken and she complained that having all the bother of a house without the husband to go with it was no fun. In point of fact she was not serious, for her pleasure lay precisely in running a house on her own just like a housewife, but she felt she must remind Rosa from time to time that they were no longer babes. Rosa, however, seemed incapable of behaving in a dignified manner even in the street; she pulled faces, laughed and turned round. Ginia could have smacked her. Yet when they went off to a dance together, Rosa was indispensable; with her easy, familiar ways and her high spirits, she made Ginia's superiority plain to the rest of the company. In that wonderful year when they began living on their own account, Ginia had soon realized that what made her different from the others was having the house to herself — Severino didn't count — and being able to live like a lady at her present age of sixteen. She let Rosa go around with her for the same reason that she wore the star in her hair, simply because it amused her. No one else in the district could be as crazy as Rosa when she wanted. She could pull everybody's leg, laughing and tossing her head back, and some evenings she did nothing but fool the whole time. And she could be as awkward as an old hen. 'What's up, Rosa?' someone remarked while they were waiting for the orchestra to start up. 'I'm scared' — and her eyes started out of her head — 'behind there I saw an old man staring at me and waiting for me outside, I'm scared'. Her partner was not convinced, 'He must be your grandfather, then!' 'Silly fool!' 'Let's dance, come on!' 'No, I tell you, I'm frightened!' Half-way round, Ginia heard Rosa's partner shout, 'You're an ignorant little fool; run away and play. Go back to the factory!' Then Rosa laughed and made everybody else laugh but as Ginia went on dancing she thought that the factory was just the sort of place for a girl like her. You had only to look at the mechanics who picked up acquaintance with them by fooling around in a similar manner.

If there was one of these around you could be quite sure that before the evening was out one of the girls would get mad or, if she was more hysterical, start weeping. They teased you just like Rosa. They were always trying to get you to go down to the meadows; it was no use talking to them, all of a sudden you had to be on the defensive. But they had their good points: some evenings they would sing and they could sing well, especially if Ferruccio came along with his guitar. He was a tall blond fellow always out of a job but his fingers were still black and rough from handling coal. It did not seem possible that those large hands could be so skilful and Ginia, who had once felt them under her armpits when they were all on their way back from the hills, carefully avoided looking at them while he was playing. Rosa told her that this Ferruccio had enquired about her on two or three occasions and Ginia had replied, 'Tell him to go and clean his nails first'. The next time she was hoping he would laugh at her but he had not even looked her way.

But a day came when Ginia emerged from the dressmaker's shop adjusting her hat, and found Rosa of all people in the doorway, who rushed up to her. 'What on earth's the matter?' 'I've run away from the factory!' They walked along the pavement together as far as the tram and Rosa did not bring the matter up again. Ginia felt irritated and did not know what to say. It was only when they got off the tram near the house that Rosa mumbled that she was afraid she was pregnant. Ginia said she was a little fool and they started arguing at the street-corner. Then it all passed off because Rosa had only frightened herself into thinking it. But Ginia in the meantime had got into much more of a state than her friend, feeling she had been cheated and left out of it as if she was a child while the rest of them had a good time, particularly by Rosa, who did not possess the least pride. 'I'm worth two of her', reflected Ginia, 'sixteen's too soon. So much the worse for her if she wants to chuck herself away'. Although she spoke like this, she was unable to think about it without feeling humiliated. She could not get over the idea that the others had gone down to the meadows without a word to her about it while she, who lived on her own, still felt thrilled at the touch of a man's hand. 'But why did you come and tell me about it that day?' she asked Rosa one afternoon when they were out together. 'And who did you expect me to tell? I was in a jam'. 'But why hadn't you ever told me anything before?' Rosa, who was quite at her ease again now, merely laughed. She changed her tactics. 'It's much nicer when you don't tell. It's bad luck to talk about it'. 'She's a fool', thought Ginia, 'she laughs now but only a short while back she was going to commit suicide. She's not grown up yet, that's what it is'. Meanwhile when she did her journeying to and fro in the street, even on her own, she thought how they were all very young and how you would have to be twenty years old all of a sudden to know how to go on.

Ginia watched Rosa's lover a whole evening, Pino with his bent nose, an undersized fellow whose only accomplishment was billiards; who never did anything and talked out of the side of his mouth. Ginia could not understand why Rosa still went to the pictures with him when she had found out what a nasty piece of work he was. She could not get that Sunday out of her head when they had all gone out in a boat together and she had noticed that Pino's back was covered with freckles as if it was rusty. Now that she knew, she recalled that Rosa had gone off with him down under the trees. She had been stupid not to see how it was. But Rosa was stupider still and she told her so once more in the cinema-entrance.

To think they had all gone in the boat so many times, had laughed and joked and the various couples lay around in each other's arms. Ginia had seen the rest of them but had failed to notice Rosa and Pino. In the hot midday sun she and Tina, the lame girl, had remained alone in the boat. The others had got out on to the bank where their shouts could be heard. Tina, who had kept on her petticoat and blouse, said to Ginia, 'If no one comes along. I shall undress and sunbathe'. Ginia said she would stand on guard but she found herself listening, instead, to the voices and silences from the shore. For a short time everything was quiet on the peaceful water. Tina had stretched herself full length in the sun with a towel round her waist. Then

Ginia had jumped down on to the grass and walked around barefooted. She could no longer hear Amelia's voice which had retreated beyond the others. Ginia, like a fool, imagining they were playing hide-and-seek, had not looked for them and had gone back to the boat.

Two

One knew that Amelia, at any rate, was leading a different kind of life. Her brother was a mechanic but she only put in an appearance now and again during the evenings of that summer; she did not confide in any of them but joined in with their laughter for no other reason than because she was in her twentieth year. Ginia envied her her build, for Amelia's legs showed off a good pair of stockings. She looked rather heavy round the hips in her bathing costume, however, and her features were faintly horsey. 'I'm unemployed', she remarked to Ginia one evening when she was having a good look at the latter's dress, 'so I have all the day before me to study my pattern. I've learnt how to cut out through working in a dressmaker's shop like you. Can you?' Ginia thought it nicer to have things specially made but did not say so. They had a stroll together that evening and Ginia accompanied her as far as her house because she felt wide-awake and sleep was out of the question. It had been raining and the asphalt and the trees had been washed clean; she felt the coolness against her cheeks.

'You like going for walks, don't you?' said Amelia, laughing. 'What does your brother Severino think about it?' 'Severino is working at this time. It's his job to switch on all the lights and generally attend to them'. 'So he's the one that floodlights all the couples, is he? What sort of a get-up does he wear – like a gasman?' 'Of course not', laughed Ginia. 'He sees to all the switches at the Central Electric Works. He stands all night in front of a machine'. 'So you two are on your own. Doesn't he ever preach at you?' Amelia spoke with the cheerful assurance of one who knew all about men's ways and Ginia felt thoroughly at ease with her. 'Have you been out of a job long?' she asked. 'I have one actually. I'm being painted'.

It sounded like a joke the way she said it and Ginia looked at her. 'Painted, how?' 'Front face, profile, dressed, undressed, I'm what's called a model'.

Ginia listened with a puzzled expression so as to draw her out though she knew exactly what Amelia meant. What seemed incredible was that she should discuss it with her, for Amelia had never alluded to the matter directly in front of any of them and it was only through the concierge that Rosa had made the discovery.

'Do you really go to a painter's studio?'

'I used to', said Amelia, 'But in summer it's cheaper for an artist to paint out of doors. In winter it's too cold to pose in the nude and so you hardly ever get a job then'. 'Do you undress then?' 'Of course', said Amelia.

Then, taking Ginia by the arm, she continued, 'It's lovely work; you've nothing to do except just stand listening to them talking. I used to go to an artist who had a magnificent studio and when visitors came, they all took tea. You can learn a lot posing among that set – more than at the pictures'.

'Did they used to come in while you were sitting?'

'They asked permission. Women painters are best. Did you know that women painted as well? They pay a girl to pose for them in the nude. I can't think why they don't just stand in front of a mirror. I could understand it if they used a man as a model'.

'But they do', said Ginia.

'I don't say they don't', said Amelia, stopping in front of the door and giving a wink. 'But they pay some models double. Bless you, variety's the spice of life'.

Ginia asked her why she did not come and call for her sometimes, and then went homeward alone, treading on the reflections she made on the asphalt road which had nearly dried in the warm night air. 'She chatters too much about her own affairs; I suppose it's being older', thought Ginia, feeling happy. 'If I led her sort of life, I'd be more discreet'. Ginia was a little disappointed when she realized the days were slipping by and Amelia had not called on her. It was clear enough that she had not been trying to make up to her that evening, which implies – reflected Ginia – that she tells everything to everybody and really is stupid. I expect she regards me as an infant in arms, ready to believe anything. One evening Ginia told a number of other girls that she had seen a picture in a shop for which Amelia had been the model.

They all believed it but what Ginia meant was that she had recognized her by her build, because artists intentionally disguise the face when the model is in the nude. 'Do you imagine they're as considerate as that?' said Rosa, jeering at her for her simplicity. 'I would be only too pleased if an artist painted me and paid me into the bargain', said Clara. Then they proceeded to discuss Amelia's looks, and Clara's brother, who had been in the boat with them, claimed that he was more handsome in the nude. They all laughed and Ginia said, 'An artist wouldn't paint her if she wasn't well set up', but they ignored her remark. She felt humiliated that evening and could have wept with rage; but the days went by and the next time she met Amelia – getting off a tram – they walked along together, chatting. Ginia was more smartly dressed than Amelia, who went along carrying her hat and showed all her teeth when she laughed.

The following afternoon Amelia came to pick her up. She walked up to the open door out of the heat and Ginia spied her from the darkness inside, without being seen herself. Once the shutters were thrown open, they took their ease and Amelia, fanning herself with her hat, looked round her. 'I like the idea of an open door', she remarked. 'You're lucky. You can't at my place because we're on the ground floor'. Then she glanced into the other room where Severino was sleeping and said, 'At our

9

place it's a regular bear-garden. Five of us – not to mention the cats – in a couple of rooms'. They went out together when they were ready and Ginia said, 'When you're fed up with your ground floor, come and join me, you can have some peace here'. She was trying to make Amelia understand that she wasn't meaning to criticize her people in any way but was just glad that the two of them were getting on together. Amelia, however, did not say either yes or no and treated her to a coffee on the way to the tram. Ginia did not see her the next day or the day after that, but she came up one evening, hatless, sat down on the sofa and with a laugh asked for a cigarette. Ginia was finishing the washing-up and Severino was shaving. He offered her a cigarette and lit it for her with his wet fingers and all three of them had a good laugh about the street-lamp business. Severino had to go off but not before telling Ginia not to stay up all night. Amelia had an amused expression on her face as she watched him go out.

'Don't you ever go to a different dance-hall?' she asked Ginia. 'Our boys are all right but they hold you too tight for my liking. Like your girl friends'.

They both went down to the town-centre without hats, choosing the shady part of the streets. They had an ice to start with and as they licked it, they watched the passers-by and joked about them. Everything came easily to Amelia; she gave herself up to having a good time as if nothing else mattered and that evening the most wonderful things might happen. Ginia knew she was safe with Amelia, who was twenty and strolled along as if she owned the place. Amelia had not even put on stockings because of the heat, and when they came to a dance-saloon, the sort that has a muffled orchestra and lamp-shades on the tables, Ginia got into a panic at the thought of having to go in with her. But her fear proved groundless and she breathed again. Then Amelia said, 'Don't you feel a desire to go in there?' 'It's too hot and we aren't dressed for it', said Ginia, 'let's go on;

it's much nicer'. 'I quite agree', said Amelia, 'but what shall we do? Don't you ever want to stand at a street-corner and laugh at the passers-by?'

'What would you like to do?'

'If we weren't women, we should have a car and by this time we would be having a bathe in the lakes'.

'Let's have a walk and a chat', suggested Ginia.

'We could go to the hills and have a drink and sing, maybe. Do you like wine?'

Ginia said she didn't and Amelia looked at the entrance to the dance-saloon. 'We'll have a drink, though. Come along! People who are bored have only themselves to blame'. They had a drink at the first café they came to, and once they had got outside again, Ginia felt a coolness in the air she had not felt before and thought how nice it was to cool your blood with drinks in the summer heat. Meanwhile Amelia began some rigmarole about how the people who did nothing all day had at least the right to relax in the evening, but there were moments when you got frightened as you saw the time slipping by and you began to be doubtful whether it was worth while doing so much gadding about. 'Don't you feel the same?'

'The only gadding about I do is going to work', said Ginia, 'I can't get much fun when I haven't even time to think about it'. 'You're only a kid', said Amelia, 'but I can't keep still even when I'm working'.

'You have to when you're posing', remarked Ginia as they walked on.

Amelia began to laugh. 'You've not got a clue. The cleverest models are the ones who drive the artists frantic. If you don't move every now and again, they forget you're a model and treat you as if you were a servant. Behave like a sheep and the wolf will eat you'.

Ginia merely smiled by way of reply, but something was on the tip of her tongue that burnt it like brandy. Then she asked

Amelia why they didn't go and sit down in the open air and have another drink. 'But of course', said Amelia. They had it at the bar because it was cheaper that way.

By this time Ginia was beginning to feel warmed up and on their way out found no difficulty in saying to Amelia, 'This is what I've been wanting to ask. I'd like to see you pose'.

They discussed the question for a short part of the walk and Amelia laughed because, dressed or undressed, a model can only be of interest to men and hardly to another girl. The model merely stands there; what is there to see? Ginia said she wanted to see the artist paint her; she had never seen anyone handling colours and it must be nice to watch. 'I don't mean today or tomorrow', she said, 'I know you're out of work at present. But if you go back to some artist's studio, you must promise to take me along with you'. Amelia laughed again and told her that as far as introducing her to artists, it was the least she could do; she knew where they lived and could take her there. 'But they're a lousy lot, you'll have to watch out'. And Ginia laughed too.

They were sitting on a bench and there were no people going by now for it was neither early nor late. They wound up the evening in a dance-saloon in the hills.

Three

After that Amelia often called for her to go out or to have a chat. She would come into the room and talk loudly, stopping Severino from getting any sleep. When Rosa came along in the afternoon, she found both of them ready to go out. If Amelia happened to be smoking she would finish her cigarette and would give advice to Rosa, who had told her about Pino. It was obvious that she did not care to stay longer than necessary in her lodgings and having nothing else to do all day, was glad of their company. And she would tease Rosa too when they were on their own, pretending she did not believe her stories and laughing at her quite openly.

Ginia confided in Amelia when she realized that, for all her high spirits, she was really pretty wretched. Ginia could see this merely by noticing her eyes and her crudely made-up mouth. Amelia went about without stockings only because she did not possess any; the nice dress she always wore was the only one she had. Ginia felt convinced she was correct in her conclusions when she realized on one occasion that she too felt more irresponsible if she went about without a hat. The person who got on her nerves was Rosa whom she had suddenly fathomed. 'Life's worth living', said Rosa, 'even if you've got to go to bed when you've torn your dress'. On various occasions Ginia asked Amelia why she didn't go back to posing for artists, and Amelia told her it was no good looking for a job once you were 'unemployed'.

How pleasant it would have been to have nothing to do all day long and go out for walks together in the cool of the day, but to be so smartly turned out that when they stared at shop-windows, people would stare at them. 'Being free in the way I am, makes me mad', said Amelia. Ginia would have gladly paid money to hear her hold forth so eagerly on many things which she liked, because real confidence consists in knowing what the other person wants and when someone else is pleased by the same things, you no longer feel in awe of her. But Ginia was not sure that when, towards evening, they went under the porticoes, Amelia was looking at the same man as she was. Nor could she ever be really sure what hat or material she liked; there was always the possibility that she would laugh at her as she did with Rosa. Although she was alone she never said what she would like to do, or if she did talk, it was never seriously. 'Have you ever noticed when you're waiting for someone', she said, 'all the ugly mugs and scraggy legs that go by? It's amusing'. Perhaps Amelia was joking but possibly she did devote the odd quarter of an hour to doing that sort of thing, and Ginia reflected that she would be very mad to confess that evening to her great desire to see an artist painting.

When they went out nowadays, it was Amelia who chose where they should go, and Ginia obligingly allowed herself to be taken in tow. They went back to the dance-hall of the other evening, but Ginia who had enjoyed herself so much on that occasion, no longer recognized either the lighting or the orchestra; the only pleasure she got was from the fresh air that came in at the open balconies. That is to say she did not feel well enough dressed to move around among the tables down below. Amelia, however, had embarked on a conversation with a young man with whom she was evidently already on familiar terms. When the band stopped, another man dived up and waved his hand and Amelia turned round and said, 'Is it you he's interested in?' Ginia was pleased to have been noticed by someone but the youth had disappeared, and an unpleasant type who had had a dance with her before passed hurriedly by without seeing her. Ginia had the impression that the first evening they had come, they had never once sat down at a table except to get their breath back, whereas now they waited some considerable time under the window, and Amelia who was the first to take her place, said in a loud voice, 'It's good fun this time too, isn't it?' Certainly no one else in the room was better dressed than Amelia and many of the women were not wearing stockings, but Ginia had a special eye for the waiters' white jackets and was impressed by the number of cars outside. Then she realized how foolish she was to hope that Amelia's artist friend might be there.

It was so hot that year that they needed to go out every evening and Ginia felt she had never known before what summer was, so pleasant was it to stroll along the avenues every night. Sometimes she thought the summer would never end and they must make haste to enjoy it together because when the season changed something was bound to happen. For this reason she no longer went to the dance-hall with Rosa or to their local cinema, but sometimes she went out on her own and hurried to the cinema in the town-centre. Why should not she do it, if Amelia did? One evening Amelia called and as they were going out, remarked, 'Yesterday I found a job'. Ginia was not surprised. She expected it. She quietly asked her if she was beginning straight away. 'I started this morning', said Amelia. 'I've already done two hours'. 'Are you pleased?' asked Ginia.

Then she enquired what sort of picture it was going to be. 'It's not a picture at all. He is just making studies. He's drawing my face. I chatter away and at intervals he dashes down a profile. It's not anything permanent'. 'So you're not posing then?' said Ginia. 'You seem to imagine', retorted Amelia, 'that posing merely consists of getting undressed and standing around'. 'Are you going back tomorrow?' said Ginia.

Amelia in point of fact went there the next day and for

several days afterwards. The following evening she referred laughingly to it and went on to talk about the artist, how he never stood still and asked her if any other painter had ever drawn her in that way before, walking up and down all the time. 'He did a nude of me this morning. He's one of those who know what they're about and arrive at their goal by gradual stages. But with four drawings they've got you taped and put away in their portfolio and have no further use for you'. Ginia asked her what he was like. Amelia said, a little man. 'How did you come across him?' It had been by chance. 'Call for me tomorrow', said Amelia. They planned to go along together the next afternoon, Saturday.

The whole length of the street in the hot sun that afternoon, Amelia had kept her in fits of laughter. They made their way by a winding staircase into a large semi-dark room which took a little sunlight only from the back through a gap in the curtains. Ginia, her heart pounding fast, had stopped on the last stair. Amelia called out, 'Good afternoon', and walked as far as the middle of the room in the half-light and a man emerged from behind the curtains, plump and with a grey goatee beard, and said, making a gesture with his hand, 'Nothing doing, girls. I'm off today'. He had donned a light-coloured overall which became a dirty yellow when he turned and drew the curtain back to let in a little light. 'It's no use my working today, girls. I need some fresh air'. Ginia had not moved from the stair. She could see Amelia's legs against the light, some distance away. Quietly she said, as if to herself, 'Let's go, Amelia'.

'Will this be the little friend who wants to meet me? But she's a mere babe. Let's see you in the light'.

Ginia climbed the last stair, reluctantly, feeling the grey inquisitive eyes fixed on her. She could not decide whether they were the eyes of an old man or a cunning old devil. She heard Amelia's voice – brusque, irritated – saying, 'But you gave us an appointment'.

'What do you want to do here?' he said. 'What in heaven's name? You are tired too. Work is a thing you've got to go at gently. Aren't you thankful to have a rest?'

Then Amelia went and sat down on a chair under the shadow of the curtain and Ginia found herself standing for what appeared an endless time not knowing how to respond to the glances she received from the two of them who stared at each other and then at her. The fellow gave her the impression that he was joking, but it was a private joke for himself alone. He was still talking to her; he spoke in jerks and kept repeating, 'What do you want to do?' Then suddenly the diminutive figure hopped back and drew the curtains still further to one side. A smell of freshly mixed gesso and varnish filled the empty studio.

'We are boiling hot', said Amelia, 'at least you can let us cool down a bit, can't he, Ginia?' As she spoke their bearded friend swung round again and opened the large skylights. Amelia who was sitting with her legs crossed, watched him and laughed. Below the window was an easel bearing a canvas covered with daubs of colour partly scraped down. 'If you don't work now while it's light, when do you work?' remarked Amelia. 'I bet you are going to let me down and have another model'. 'I let down everybody in existence', shouted the painter, lowering his chin. 'Do you consider yourself any more valuable than a horse or a plant? It's work for me even when I am out walking, can't you understand that?' Meanwhile he rummaged about in a chest under the easel and threw out some sheets of paper, some small boxes of colour and some brushes. Amelia jumped up from her seat, removed her hat and winked at Ginia. 'Why don't you sketch my friend?' she asked laughingly. 'She's never sat for anyone before'. The painter turned round. 'All right, I will', he said, 'she's got an interesting face'.

He began to walk round Ginia, keeping a short distance away, his head turned towards her. In one hand he held a pencil and with the other he stroked his beard, staring at her all the time like a cat. Ginia who was in the centre of the studio did not dare move. Then he directed her to stand in the light, and without taking his eyes off her, threw a sheet of paper on to the easel board and began to draw. A yellow cloud could be seen in the sky and some roofs of houses; Ginia fixed her eyes on the cloud. Her heart was thumping hard. She heard Amelia make some remark; she could also hear the sound of her footsteps and her rapid breathing, but she did not turn to look.

When Amelia gave her a shout to come and see the drawing, Ginia had to close her eyes to get accustomed to the semi-darkness. Then she quietly bent over the paper and recognized her hat, but her face looked like someone else's; a dreamy face, expressionless, the lips parted as if she was talking in her sleep. 'A kind of abstracted look', said Barbetta, 'Is it true that no one has ever drawn you before?' He got her to remove her hat and told her to sit down and chat with Amelia. As they sat there looking at each other, they felt a great desire to burst out laughing. The artist went on covering more sheets of paper. Amelia signed to Ginia, telling her to forget she was posing.

'Abstracted', repeated Barbetta, looking at her from the side. 'One would say that the virgin profile is not yet resolved into a definite form'. Ginia asked Amelia if she was not going to pose too and Amelia slowly replied, 'You're his discovery today. He will certainly hang on to you'.

While they were talking, Ginia asked her if they could see the drawings he had done of her on previous occasions. Then Amelia rose and looked out a portfolio at the back of the room. She opened it on her knees, saying, 'Have a look!' Ginia turned over several sheets; at the fourth or fifth, she was in a cold sweat. She did not dare to say anything, feeling the grey eyes of the man behind her. Amelia, too, was looking at her expectantly, and said finally, 'Do you like them?'

Ginia raised her head, forcing a smile, 'I don't recognize you', she said. She proceeded to turn them over, one by one. By the time she had finished, she was more composed. After all Amelia was there in front of her, with her clothes on and smiling.

She remarked, feeling an idiot, 'Did he do them?' Amelia, baffled, replied, 'I certainly didn't!'

When Barbetta had finished the next batch, Ginia would have liked to have waited a little while with her eyes closed as they were dazzled by the light outside. But Amelia shouted to her to come and Ginia was astonished when she looked at the large sheet of paper in front of her. There were lots of drawings of her head, dashed down all over the sheet, some distorted, some showing an expression which she had certainly never worn, but the hair, cheeks, nostrils were true to life and definitely recognisable as hers. She turned to Barbetta, who was laughing; she could not believe they were the same grey eyes of a little time back.

Then he had been letting fly at Amelia who began abusing him and insisting that an hour was an hour and that Ginia worked for a living. She repeated that she had just come along with her casually, without any intention of stealing her job. Barbetta laughed between his teeth and said he must leave them. 'Come along, I'll buy you an ice. But then I'm off'.

Four

They returned there together next morning. This time it was Amelia's turn to pose. 'Look out for yourself', said Amelia, 'if you take my place again. That scoundrel knows you are partial to ices and is ready to exploit that virgin business'. Ginia did not feel as pleased as she had on the previous occasion and as soon as she was awake, she had thought about the sketches of herself all amongst the nudes of Amelia and how worked up she had been. She nursed the hope of getting him to give her the drawings, not so much from a wish to possess them as because she did not like the idea of them lying there among all the others for anyone to gape at. She could not convince herself that Barbetta, that plump, pompous old artist, had drawn, rubbed out, squared up Amelia's legs, back, belly and breasts. He daren't look her in the face. Those grey eyes and that lead pencil had fixed, measured and scrutinized her more shamelessly than a mirror and put an end to her gaiety and chatter.

'I hope I am not disturbing you this morning', she said as they passed through the doorway. 'Look here', said Amelia, 'do you, or do you not want to see me pose? Another time I'll be careful to keep clear of respectable girls'.

All the studio windows were open and the curtains drawn back and while they were waiting for Barbetta, the old servant emerged from the stairway to come and keep an eye on them. Ginia wondered whether Amelia was getting ready to sit but she could hear her arguing with the old servant and getting her to close the windows because the morning air was chilling the room. The old woman mumbled rather than spoke, her face was so scruffy and hairy that Amelia was laughing at it, quite openly.

At length Barbetta arrived, putting on his overall and rushing around. The easel was moved to the back of the studio and his palette was brought in. There was a divan-bed at the far end and they drew all the curtains except the last one so that all the light fell on to that corner. Ginia felt *de trop* in all the turmoil and she got the impression that the old woman was looking at her disapprovingly.

When the latter left the room, Amelia began undressing near the divan and Ginia began to watch Barbetta's large hand. He held a thin piece of charcoal between his fingers and he was putting in a dark background on a sheet of whitish paper pinned on the easel. Without so much as a look in her direction, Barbetta told her to sit down, and she could hear Amelia saying something. Ginia gazed through the skylight on to the roofs as if she were posing again and thought how stupid she was. She made an effort and turned round.

Her first reaction was that Amelia must be feeling cold, that Barbetta hardly seemed to be looking at her and that it was she herself who was the nuisance, coming along like that out of curiosity. Amelia, a brunette, somehow looked dirty and she found difficulty in keeping her eyes on her. She was sitting on the divan with her arms against the back of a chair, her face turned away and displaying the whole of her leg and thigh and right up to her armpit. Ginia got bored after a while. She watched Barbetta rubbing out and redrawing, saw his brow wrinkled with concentration, exchanged a smile with Amelia – but she still felt bored. But her heart began to beat again when Amelia got up for the first time to stretch herself and picked up her bathing slip which had fallen off the divan. It was the sort of foolish excitement she would have felt if they had been alone, the excitement at the discovery that they were both made in the same mould and whoever had seen

Amelia naked was really seeing *her*. She began to feel terribly ill at ease.

From her head that was resting on her arm came Amelia's voice, 'Hello, Ginia'. It was enough to please and calm her. A moment before she had noticed a red mottling on Amelia's leg and wondered whether if she stripped, she would have markings like that. 'But my skin is younger', she said. Then she asked aloud, 'Has he ever painted you in colour?' It was Barbetta who replied, 'Colours are not accurate. They come in the window with the sunlight. Colours do not exist indoors'. 'Naturally', interpolated Amelia, 'you're too mean. Colours cost money!' 'Excuse me!' shouted the old man, 'the reason is that I have a proper respect for colour and you know nothing at all about it beyond the colour you smear on your lips. This blonde here knows more about it than you'. Amelia shrugged her shoulders but without shifting her head.

The sound of a siren came from somewhere beyond the roof-tops and Ginia began to stroll round. She discovered the portrait sketches of her on the window-sill but had not the courage to ask for them. As she looked through them she saw those of Amelia again and eyed them rapidly, wondering if Amelia had really assumed the poses shown, some of which almost suggested acrobatic feats. Was it possible that an old man like Barbetta could still get a kick out of sketching girls and studying their anatomy? He was badly bitten, too, she thought.

They left after twelve o'clock and were pleased to find themselves among people again and walk along properly dressed and see the lovely colours in the street which came from the sun – it was undeniable, though they did not know how – since they disappeared at night. Even Amelia's edginess had vanished and she paid for the apéritif and they dropped the subject of painters.

Ginia's thoughts turned back to them, alone on her sofa, that afternoon and others as well. Once more she saw Amelia's swarthy belly in that semi-darkness, that very ordinary face and those drooping breasts. Surely a woman offered a better subject dressed? If painters wanted to do them in the nude, they must have ulterior motives. Why did they not draw from male models? Even Amelia when disgracing herself in that way became a different person; Ginia was almost in tears.

But she mentioned nothing about it to Amelia and was merely glad that the latter was at present earning again, that she was with her once more and was quite keen to accompany her to the cinema. Amelia could now buy herself some stockings and began to take more trouble over her hair. Ginia found it a real pleasure to be going out with her again because Amelia was such a striking figure and many people turned round to have another look at her. Thus the summer drew to a close and one evening Amelia said, 'Your Barbetta man is going into the country to find his colours and do some harvesting. I was beginning to find him irritating'.

That evening Amelia had produced a new handbag and Ginia remarked, 'Is that his parting gift?' '*Hira!*' said Amelia, 'don't make me laugh! It's you he would like to have back so he wouldn't need to pay'.

Then they quarrelled because Amelia had kept all this back so far and now both of them were so outspoken that they parted on bad terms. 'So, she's found a lover', thought Ginia as she went home alone, 'she's found a lover who is giving her presents'. She decided she would only make up their quarrel if Amelia came and begged her to.

Reluctantly and in defence against her boredom, Ginia tried to pick up with her former friends again. After all, by the following summer she would be seventeen and she felt she knew her way around as much as Amelia, the more so now she was out of touch with her. During the evenings, already becoming cold, she tried to put on an Amelia-act with Rosa. She often laughed openly at her and took her for long, chatty walks. She talked to her about Pino, but she had not the nerve to take her to the dance-saloon in the hills.

Amelia had certainly someone in tow; no one ever saw her. 'As long as a woman has plenty of clothes', thought Ginia, 'she can cut a dash. The main thing is not to let herself be seen in the nude'. But she could not discuss that sort of thing either with Rosa or Clara or with their brothers, who would immediately have drawn the worst conclusion and tried to paw her about, and Ginia did not want that; she had realized now that there were better people in the world than Ferruccio or Pino. In the evenings when she was with them, they would dance and joke and chat as well, but Ginia knew that it was no different from the larking round on Sundays when they went in the boat; a light-hearted bit of fun among the lads – the effect of the sun and their singing – when it only needed one of their number to drape a towel round his waist and pretend to be a woman to set them off into fits of laughter. At present, however, the Sunday evenings were a source of irritation because Ginia on her own was unable to make up her mind and let herself be taken along with the others. She found occasional amusement in the shop when the boss required her to do the pinning on a customer's dress; some of the stories told by the more eccentric customers were so funny. It was still more amusing when her boss affected to believe them quite seriously while all the time the mirrors reflected back the malicious mockery in her face. On one occasion a young blonde arrived who gave the impression of having a car waiting for her, but if she really had, thought Ginia, she would certainly have gone to a better-class dressmaker's. She was a tall young woman but looked evasive. Ginia considered her handsome, yes, even just in her knickers and brassière she was slim and handsome. She would certainly have made a lovely picture if she had sat for an artist; perhaps she was a model, for she paraded in front of the mirrors with the same deportment as Amelia. The next day Ginia saw the invoice but as it only had her surname on it, she was no wiser. As far as she was concerned the blonde lady continued to be a model. One evening Ginia was invited in by a friend of Severino who came to the house to bring her a lamp. The next day she went to his shop. He was a young chap like Severino and she was not in awe of him because he always wore his overalls and some years before he used to take hold of her wrists and ask her if she'd like to be whirled round. Now he looked at her with his tongue between his teeth. Ginia went there because Amelia's door could be seen from his shop, but Massimo certainly had no idea why she stopped for a chat and a joke and then returned next day as well.

They were looking at the red and blue lamps and she was playing the fool. They could see people passing by through the shop-window and Ginia asked him if it was true that Amelia went about in a white dress. 'How should I know?' asked Massimo. 'There's such a gang of you girls. Severino will know'. 'Why Severino?' 'Severino is fond of fillies. Is it the girl who goes about without stockings?' 'Did he tell you?' asked Ginia. 'What, you his sister and don't know?' replied Massimo with a laugh. 'Get Amelia to tell you. Doesn't she still come to your place?'

This was all news to Ginia. The idea that Severino was sweet on Amelia, that they had talked about it and had been seeing each other ruined her day. If it was true, all Amelia's 'crush' on her had been put on. 'I'm just a kid', thought Ginia, and to contain her anger, she remembered how disgusted she had been seeing her in the nude. 'But is it true?' she wondered; she found it impossible to imagine Severino in love with anyone, and she was certain that if he had seen her posing that time, poor Amelia would have lost her appeal for him. 'But would she in fact? But why have we to be nude?' she thought despairingly.

Towards evening she began to feel calmer and persuaded

herself that Massimo had said it merely for something to say. When she was at table with Severino, she looked at his hands and broken nails, knowing that Amelia was used to something very different. Then she remained alone when the lights were out and her mind went back to the wonderful August evenings when Amelia used to come and call for her. Just then she heard her voice at the door.

Five

'I've come to look you out', said Amelia.

At first Ginia did not reply.

'Are you still angry with me?' asked Amelia. 'Let bygones be bygones. Isn't your brother here?'

'He is out at the moment.'

Amelia was wearing her old dress but her hair was well styled and had coral combs in it. She went and sat down on the sofa and suddenly asked her if she was going out. She spoke in the same tone of voice as of old but it was huskier, as if she had a cold.

'Is it me you want or Severino?' asked Ginia.

'Oh, those people. Take no notice what they say. I only want to be distracted, are you coming along?'

Then Ginia changed her stockings and they hurried down and Amelia got her to tell her all the month's news.

'What have you been up to?' asked Ginia. 'What do you think?' replied Amelia, beginning to laugh, 'nothing at all. This evening I said, "Let's go and see if Ginia is still thinking about Barbetta"'. She could not pump any more out of her, but Ginia was satisfied. 'What about going to have some refreshments?' she suggested.

While they were having a drink, Amelia asked her why she had never come and dug her out. 'I didn't know where to find you'. 'Where do you expect? At the café all day long'. 'You'd never told me'.

Next day Ginia went to find her at the café. It was a new café under the porticoes and Ginia searched round to find her. It was Amelia finally who hailed her in a loud voice as if she were in her own house, and Ginia saw that she was wearing a smart grey coat and a hat with a veil which made her almost unrecognisable. She was sitting with her legs crossed, resting her chin on one fist as if she were posing. 'Did you really want to come?' she smiled.

'Are you expecting somebody?' enquired Ginia.

'I always am', said Amelia, making room for her next to her.

'It's my job. You've got to queue up for the privilege of stripping in front of an artist'.

Amelia had a newspaper on the table and a packet of cigarettes. She was evidently earning. 'I like your hat but it makes you look old', said Ginia, looking her in the eyes. 'I am old', said Amelia, 'any objections?'

Amelia was leaning back against the mirror as if she was on a sofa. She was looking in front of her at the mirror opposite in which Ginia could also see herself, lower down. They might have been mother and daughter. 'Are you always here?' she asked. 'Do artists come?'

'They come when they feel inclined. There hasn't been one today'.

The chandelier was illuminated and lots of people were passing by the window. Although there was plenty of cigarette smoke round about them, it was so quiet that the buzz of conversation and other sounds seemed to reach them from a long way off. Ginia noticed two girls in a corner holding court and talking to the waiter. 'Are they models?' she said.

'I don't know', replied Amelia. 'Will you take coffee or an apéritif?'

Ginia had always thought one should go into cafés with a male escort and she was surprised that Amelia should spend her afternoons there alone, but she found it so pleasant to get away from the shop, stroll round the arcades and have somewhere to go, that she betook herself there again the next day. If she could have been sure that Amelia liked seeing her, she would have really enjoyed it. This time Amelia caught sight of her through the café window and made a sign that she was coming outside. They took a tram together.

Amelia did not say much that evening. 'They're a lot of louts', was about all she said. 'Were you waiting for someone?' asked Ginia.

In the course of their parting remarks, they planned for the following day and Ginia felt convinced that Amelia liked seeing her and that if something had gone wrong, it had been for other reasons, possibly something to do with the 'uncouth louts'.

'How does it work? Does an artist come along and ask you if you are willing to sit?' she asked, laughing.

'There are some, too, who don't say anything', explained Amelia. 'They don't need models'.

'What do they paint then?'

'Do you know what! There's one artist who says that he applies paint as we apply lipstick! "What do you paint when you're putting on lipstick? Well, I paint the same way", he says'.

'But you paint your lips with lipstick'.

'And he paints his canvas. Bye-bye, Ginia'.

When Amelia talked in this mocking way with a straight face Ginia was afraid something was afoot and felt uneasy and lonely as she went home. Luckily for her, once there, she had to hurry and knock up a supper of pasta for Severino. When supper was over, it was different because night was approaching and the time for going out by herself or with Rosa. Sometimes she thought, 'What sort of life am I leading? I'm always on the hop'. But it was the sort of life she liked because this was the only way she could enjoy that moment's peace in the afternoon or in the evening at Amelia's café and relax. If she had not had Amelia, she would have been less tied but how could she do what she wanted now the days were no use to her and she found no more pleasure walking down the street? And it was sure to be through Amelia and not through any of the silly fools like Rosa or Clara if anything exciting did happen that winter.

She began to pick up acquaintances at the café. There was one gentleman who resembled Barbetta and when they left, he waved his hand to Amelia. He addressed them respectfully, and Amelia told Ginia that he was not a painter. A tall young man, who drew his car up in front of the arcades and was accompanied by a very smart woman, sometimes came to the bar. Amelia did not know him but said he was not a painter.

'There don't seem to be many about, do there?' she said to Ginia. 'The ones who work seriously haven't time to come'. So Amelia had more acquaintances among waiters than among the customers but Ginia, who was fond of hearing the latter joking together, was careful not to trust any of them too far. One who often sat with Amelia and had moved to Ginia on the first occasion without so much as a glance in her direction, was a hairy youth with a white tie and very black eyes, called Rodrigues. In fact he did not look like an Italian at all and he had a peculiar, rasping voice. Amelia talked to him as if he was a naughty boy, telling him that, if instead of squandering that lira at the café, he had kept it, he could – in ten days – have paid for a model. Ginia listened, amused, but Rodrigues now began in his hesitant voice to treat Amelia alternately as a fine lady and a spoilt child. She smiled, but sometimes she was annoyed and told him to go away. Rodrigues then moved to another table, pulled out his pencil and began to write, watching them out of the corner of his eye. 'Don't pay any attention to him', said Amelia, 'it's just what he'd like'. So gradually Ginia got accustomed to ignoring him.

One evening they went out together with no particular aim in view. They had been for a walk; it had begun to rain and they took shelter under a doorway. They found it chilly standing still in their wet stockings. Amelia had said, 'If Guido is at home, what about going along to his place?' 'Who is Guido?'

Amelia had then put her nose outside and craned her neck to look at the windows of the house opposite. 'There's a light; let's go up, we shall be under cover'. They had mounted at least to the sixth floor and had reached the attics when Amelia paused, breathless, and said, 'Are you afraid?' 'Why should I be?' said Ginia, 'You know him, don't you?'

While they were knocking at the door, they could hear the sound of laughter inside; it was a subdued and unpleasant laugh that reminded Ginia of Rodrigues. They heard footsteps, the door opened, but they could not see anyone. 'May we come in?' said Amelia.

It was Rodrigues. He was lying on a sofa against the wall under a harsh light. But there was someone else there, standing up; it was a soldier in his shirt sleeves, blond, mud-stained, who looked at them and smiled. Ginia had to lower her eyes against the glare of the lamp, which appeared to be acetylene. Three of the walls were covered with pictures and curtains but the fourth consisted entirely of windows.

Amelia said to Rodrigues in a tone that was half serious, half amused, 'So it is you, after all!' He waved his hand by way of greeting and shouted: 'The other girl is called Ginia, Guido'. The soldier then shook hands with her, looking her over with an impudent smile on his face.

Ginia realized that the situation required self-possession on her part, and allowed her eyes to wander above Amelia's and Guido's heads to the pictures on the wall; they seemed to be mostly landscapes with plains and mountains but she also caught a glimpse of some portraits. The lamp that hung without a shade, such as one sees in incompleted houses, dazzled her without providing an adequate light. By looking hard, she could see that there were fewer curtains than at Barbetta's, though there was a red one which shut off the room at the back and Ginia concluded there must be another room beyond it.

Guido asked if they would care for a drink. A bottle and

31

some glasses stood on the large table in the middle of the room. 'We've come up to get warm', said Amelia. 'We're drenched up to our knees'. Guido poured out drinks – it was red wine – and Amelia took a glass over to Rodrigues, who left his recumbent position to sit up. While they were drinking, Amelia said to him, 'If Guido doesn't object, I would be glad if, now that you're up, you would let me have the bed to warm up my legs in. Beds are for women. You come too, Ginia!' But Ginia did not wish to and said that the wine had warmed her up and sat down on a chair. Then Amelia removed her shoes and her jacket and threw herself under the bed-cover. Rodrigues remained sitting on the edge of the sofa as before.

'Go on with the conversation', said Amelia. 'But this light's worrying me'. She stretched out her arm up the wall and turned it out. 'That's that. Give me a cigarette'.

Ginia sat in the dark, terrified. But she realized that Guido had gone over to the sofa, heard him striking a match and saw the two faces in the flame and the darting shadow. Then darkness again, and for a few seconds no sound of breathing. You could just hear the rain dripping under the windows.

Someone broke the silence for a moment but Ginia who still felt ill at ease, did not catch the words. She noticed that Guido was smoking too and quietly pacing up and down in the dark. She could see the glow of his cigarette and hear his footsteps. She next became aware that Amelia and Rodrigues were having a tiff. It was only when she had gradually got used to the darkness and was beginning to distinguish the table, the shadow of the other people and even a few of the pictures on the wall that she felt less worried. Amelia was talking to Guido about an occasion when she had been ill and had slept on the sofa. 'But you hadn't this friend in those days', she said, 'eh, what are you doing, stripping?'

It was all so strange to Ginia that she said, 'It's like being at the pictures'.

'Except you don't have to pay for a ticket', remarked Rodrigues from his corner.

Guido was still walking up and down and seemed to be everywhere at once; the thin floor vibrated under his boots. They were all talking at once but Ginia suddenly noticed that Amelia was silent, though she saw the cigarette, and that Rodrigues was silent as well. There was only Guido's voice filling the room, explaining something, she could not make out what, because her ear was against the sofa. A light from the lamps outside came through the windows like a reflection from the rain and she could hear the rain splashing and pouring on to the roofs and guttering. Every time both the rain and the voices ceased, it somehow seemed colder. Then Ginia strained her eyes into the darkness trying to see Amelia's cigarette.

Six

Now that it had stopped raining, they said goodbye at the door down in the street. Ginia was still seeing the studio, untidy, dripping with water, in the light of the lamp. Guido had relit it several times, to pour out drinks or to hunt for something and Amelia had shaded her eyes, shouting to him from the sofa to turn it off, and she had noticed too, Rodrigues curled up against the wall at Amelia's feet, motionless.

'Haven't those two got anyone to do the room for them?' Ginia had enquired on their way back home. Amelia had replied that Guido was too independent to leave the studio key with Rodrigues.

'Did Guido paint those pictures?'

'If I was in his shoes, I would be afraid that dago would sell them and sublet the room into the bargain!'

'Have you ever posed for Guido?'

As they walked along, Amelia told her how she had got to know Rodrigues in earlier days when she was sitting for some artist or other, and Rodrigues had turned up, as he had now, and sat down in the studio as if it were a café. He had squatted in a corner of the room and had looked from her to the picture without saying a word. Even in those days he had affected a white tie. He had behaved in a like manner with another model she knew.

'But doesn't he himself ever paint?'

'Who do you think would be rash enough to stand in front of him in the nude?'

Ginia would have liked to have another look at Guido's pictures because she knew that the colours would only be seen properly by daylight. If she could have been sure that Rodrigues was out, she would have taken her courage in both hands and gone there alone. She pictured herself going upstairs, knocking at the door and finding Guido in his soldier's trousers and laughing at him, to break the ice. The attractive thing about him as a painter was that he did not seem like a painter at all. Ginia remembered how he had held out his hand with an encouraging smile, and then his voice in the dark room and his face when the light was turned up and he had looked at her as if they were a couple on their own, nothing to do with the others. But Guido would not be there now and she would have to cope with the other man.

Next day at the café she asked Amelia whether Guido would at any rate be off duty on Sunday. 'A while back you could have asked me', said Amelia, 'but I've not seen him for some time now'. 'Rodrigues has invited me to his studio whenever I care to go'. 'You want to look out!' said Amelia.

But for several days they did not see him at the café. 'What do you bet he's expecting us to go and look him out, now that he has a bed available, just to create and to see us again? It would be just like him', said Amelia.

'It's a mess', said Ginia.

Thinking it over in her mind, she was convinced that Amelia's action of getting into bed and turning out the light in front of the others was not after all such a shame-faced business; Guido and Rodrigues had scarcely taken any notice of it. What worried her was the thought of what Amelia might have done on that bed in the old days when Guido had been the sole tenant.

'How old is Guido?' she asked.

'He used to be the same age as me'.

But Rodrigues was not to be seen, and one morning while she was out shopping, Ginia passed down the street of that night. Looking up, she recognized the triangular façade of the studio. Without giving it much thought, she ran up the staircase – which seemed endless – but when she had got into the last corridor, she saw various doors and was unable to decide which was his. She realized that Guido couldn't be very important – there wasn't even a visiting card pinned on his door, and as she went down again, she thought sympathetically of him having to have the glaring lamp of that evening which must be a handicap as far as a painter was concerned. She made no reference to her visit next time she saw Amelia.

One day when they were chatting, she asked her why men became artists. 'Because some people buy pictures', retorted Amelia. 'Not all', said Ginia, 'what about the pictures that nobody buys?'

'It's a matter of taste like any other job', said Amelia. 'But they don't get much to eat'.

'They paint because they get satisfaction out of it', said Ginia.

'Listen here, would you make yourself a dress if you weren't going to wear it? Rodrigues is the sly one: he gives himself out as a painter but nobody's ever seen a paint-brush in his hand!'

That day in point of fact he was at the café, drawing in a sketch-book with great concentration. 'What are you drawing?' asked Amelia and took the book from him. Ginia had a glance, too, full of curiosity, but all she could see was an intricate network of lines which might have been a man's bronchial tubes. 'What is it? A lettuce?' asked Amelia. Rodrigues said neither yes nor no, and then they turned over the pages of the sketch-book, which was filled with drawings; some looked like skeletons of plants, some like faces without any eyes, only areas of black hatching, and others, you could not tell whether they were faces or landscapes.

'They are subjects seen at night by gaslight', said Amelia. Rodrigues laughed and Ginia felt embarrassed rather than irritated.

'Nothing worth looking at here', said Amelia, 'if you made me look like that in a portrait, I'd cut you dead'.

Rodrigues looked at her but said nothing.

'A good model is wasted on you', said Amelia. 'Where the dickens do you find models?'

'I don't use models', said Rodrigues, 'I've too great a respect for my materials'.

At this point Ginia told him she would like to see Guido's pictures again. Rodrigues replaced his sketch-book in his pocket and replied, 'At your service'. The result was that they went along the first available Sunday and Ginia missed a part of mass to be in time. They had agreed to meet in the porch but Ginia found no one there and so she went upstairs alone. Once again she hesitated among the four doors of the corridor, could not decide which one it was, and descended half the staircase, then decided she was being stupid and went up again and stood listening in front of the last door. Meanwhile a woman emerged from another; she was unkempt and wearing a dressing-gown, she had a bucket in her hand. Ginia only just managed to get up to her in time to ask her where the painter lived. But the woman did not deign either to glance at her or reply and hurried off down the corridor. Ginia, flushed and trembling, held her breath until everything was quiet again and then hurried downstairs.

Every so often someone would enter or leave by the front door and look at her in passing. Ginia began to walk up and down, feeling desperate, especially as a butcher-boy was leaning against a doorpost at the other side of the street, leering at her most unpleasantly. She thought of enquiring where the studio was of the female concierge but now she might as well wait for Amelia. It was almost midday.

To make matters worse, she had not fixed any rendezvous with Amelia and so she would have to stay on her own that afternoon. 'Nothing seems to go right for me', she thought.

Just then Rodrigues appeared in the doorway and beckoned to her. 'Amelia is up there', he said casually, 'and wants you to come up'.

Ginia accompanied him upstairs in silence. It turned out to be the last door; it had been silent within. Amelia was sitting on the sofa, smoking as if she were at the café. 'Why didn't you come up?' she asked suddenly in a quiet voice. Ginia told her not to be silly, but she and Rodrigues seemed so categorical that they expected her to find her way up that she found it impossible to argue and she could not even say that she had listened at the door – that would have made matters worse. But she had only to recall how quiet the two of them had been to realize that the sofa could tell a tale. 'They take me for an idiot', she reflected, and tried to decide whether Amelia's hair was ruffled and read the expression in Rodrigues' eyes.

Amelia's hat – the one with the veil – had been flung down on the table. Rodrigues, standing with his back to the window, was staring at her ironically. 'Perhaps a veil would suit Ginia', remarked Amelia point-blank.

Ginia frowned and, from where she stood, began to survey the pictures above Amelia's head. But all those little paintings had lost interest for her. Lifting her nose, she could detect Amelia's perfume in the cold mustiness. She could not recollect the smell of the room from the last occasion.

Then she walked through the room, looking at the pictures on the walls. She inspected a landscape, then a plate of fruit; she stopped; she could not bring herself to look away; nobody spoke. There were some female portraits; she did not recognize the faces. She came to the back of the room and found herself before the high curtain made of some heavy material such as draped the walls. It occurred to her that Guido had collected the glasses from behind there and she said, 'May I?'

in an undertone, but neither of them heard because Rodrigues was saying something. Then Ginia parted the curtain to look, but all that met her eyes was an unmade bed and the sink-recess. Behind there too she could smell Amelia's perfume and she thought it must be pleasant to sleep alone tucked away in that corner.

Seven

'Rodrigues is dying for you to sit for him', remarked Ginia, on their way home.

'So what?'

'Didn't you notice how he was hopping round you, looking at your legs?'

'Let him!' said Amelia.

'Have you ever posed for Guido?'

'Never', said Amelia.

On their way across the piazza, they saw Rosa go by, arm in arm with someone who was not Pino. She was clinging to him as if she were lame, and Ginia said, 'Look, they're afraid of losing each other!' 'You can do anything on Sundays', said Amelia. 'But surely not in the piazza. It makes you a laughing-stock'. 'All depends what you want', Amelia replied, 'if you're silly enough and want to, you can do what you like'.

Ginia had learnt from Rodrigues that Guido came and spent lots of his off-duty afternoons in the studio, painting. 'He would paint in the night, if he could', Rodrigues had remarked. 'A canvas in front of him is like a red rag to a bull. He has to go for it – and cover it!' And he had begun to laugh in his throaty voice.

Without saying a word to anyone, Ginia chose an afternoon when Rodrigues was at the café and went to the studio alone. This time again, her heart beat wildly as she went up – but for a different reason. She did not pause to reflect in front of the door which she found open. 'Come in!' shouted Guido.

Ginia banged the door behind her in her embarrassment. She stopped breathless before Guido's gaze. Perhaps it was just an evening-effect, but the velvet curtain, catching a ray of sunlight, suffused the whole room with pink. Guido moved towards her, his head down, and said, 'What do you want?'

'Don't you know me any longer?'

Guido was in his shirt sleeves as usual and in his grey-green trousers.

'What about your friend?' he said.

Then Ginia explained that she was on her own and Amelia was staying behind at the café. 'Rodrigues told me I could come and see the pictures. We came one morning before but you weren't in'.

'Sit down, then', said Guido, 'I'm finishing something'.

He went to a place near the window and began scraping a wooden board with a palette-knife. Ginia sat down on the sofa; it was so low, she felt she was falling off. His free-and-easy manner embarrassed her and a smile escaped her at the thought that all of them, painters and mechanics, were familiar like this from the start. But how pleasant it was, half-closing one's eyes in that soft light.

Guido made some remark about Amelia. 'We are friends', replied Ginia, 'but I work in a dressmaker's shop'.

The light was beginning to fade in the room, and Ginia stood up and turned to look at a picture. It was the one depicting slices of melon which looked transparent and juicy. Ginia realized that the pink light in the picture was not just the reflection of the sunlight; it echoed the red of the velvet when she had first come in. She then understood that painters had to know about such things, but she did not dare mention it to Guido. He stole up behind her and looked at the pictures with her.

'Old stuff', he said at intervals.

'But they are lovely', said Ginia, with her heart in her mouth, because from one minute to the next she was expecting to feel a hand on her back. 'They're lovely', she repeated, stepping to one side. Guido looked at the pictures but did not move.

While Guido was lighting his cigarette, Ginia, leaning against the table, began to ask him who were the subjects of the portraits and whether he had ever painted Amelia. 'She's an artists' model', she added. But Guido suddenly came to earth and said it was news to him. 'I've seen her sit', she went on. 'I certainly did not know. Who's the artist?' 'I don't know his name but she posed all right'. 'In the nude?' asked Guido. 'Yes'.

Then Guido began to laugh. 'She's found her métier, then. She's always been fond of showing her legs. Are you a model too?' 'No, I go to work', said Ginia sharply, 'at a dressmaker's'.

But she was slightly offended all the same that Guido had not suggested doing her portrait. If Barbetta had liked her profile, why shouldn't Guido?

'Amelia can tell lots of stories', she said, 'she's up to all sorts of capers. I can't make out what her game is'.

'It would be fun to get together, all of us, sometime', said Guido, 'this studio has seen some goings-on in its time'.

'It still does', said Ginia. 'Amelia and Rodrigues did not waste much time'.

Guido gave her a half-serious, half-mocking look. It was already getting dark and it was not easy to see his expression. Ginia waited for a reply that did not come. After a long silence Guido said, 'I like you Ginetta. I like you because you don't smoke. All the girls who smoke seem to suffer from some complication or other . . .'

'There's none of that smell of varnish here that you get in other painters' studios', said Ginia.

Guido got up and began to slip on his jacket. 'It's turps. A good smell'. Ginia did not know how, but suddenly she saw him in front of her and felt a hand on the nape of her neck, and all she could do, like a fool, was open her eyes wide and bang her hip against the table. Red as a live coal, she heard Guido close to her, saying, 'The scent you have under your arms is nicer than turpentine'.

Ginia thrust him from her, found the door and bolted. She did not stop until she reached the tram. After supper she went to the cinema so as to take her mind off that afternoon, but the more she thought about it, the more she knew that she would go back. That was why she felt so much in despair. She knew she had been foolish in a way that a woman of her age should not be. She could only hope that Guido was offended and would not attempt to hug her again. She could have kicked herself, for when Guido had called out something to her from the top of the stairs, she had not listened to hear whether he was asking her to come back. The whole evening in the darkness of the cinema, she thought with a heavy heart that, whatever she might decide now, she would end by going back there. She knew that this longing to see him again and to ask his forgiveness and tell him she had been a fool would drive her mad.

Ginia did not go along next day but washed under her arms and scented herself all over. She was convinced that it was her fault if she had excited him, but sometimes she felt glad she had had the nerve because now she knew what made men amorous. 'That's the sort of thing Amelia knows all about', she reflected, 'but she must have gone pretty far in the process'.

She found Amelia and Rodrigues at the café together. As soon as she had gone in, she was afraid they knew all about it, for Amelia gave her a look, but Ginia soon calmed down and affected to be tired and in a bad mood. She was thinking of Guido's voice all the time she was listening to Rodrigues trot out all the usual nonsense. Many things had now become clear to her; why, for example, Rodrigues bent over Amelia when he was talking to her, why Amelia closed her eyes like a cat, why Amelia seemed to be so thick with him. 'He has all man's appetites', she thought, 'he is worse than Guido, Amelia'. And she could not help laughing as one laughs when one is alone.

Next day she went back to the studio. That morning at the dressmaker's, Signora Bice had drily remarked that they could stay at home that afternoon because of the *festa*. At home she had found Severino changing his shirt ready for the rally. It was a patriotic festival; banners were hung out and Ginia had asked him, 'I wonder if the soldiers will have some leave of absence?' 'I'd rather they let me have some sleep', remarked Severino. But Ginia, happy, had not waited either for Amelia or Rosa to pick her up and had gone off alone. Then when she was at the studio doorway she regretted she had not gone with Amelia.

'I'll go along for a minute and see if I can find Amelia', she said to herself and stole upstairs quietly. She did not really think that Amelia would be there because at that hour she knew she would be under the porticoes. But when she got to the door and paused to get her breath, she heard Rodrigues' voice.

Eight

The door was open and it was possible to see through to the skylight. Rodrigues' voice was loud and insistent. Ginia leaned forward and saw Guido propped up against the table, listening. 'May I come in?' she whispered but they did not hear her. Guido in a grey-green shirt looked like a workman. His eyes were fixed on her but they did not seem to be seeing her. 'I was looking for Amelia', said Ginia in a thin voice.

Rodrigues had stopped talking by this time and Ginia saw him on the sofa with one knee clasped between his hands, staring. 'Isn't Amelia here?'

'This isn't the café!' said Rodrigues.

Ginia looked at Guido and hesitated. She saw him supporting himself against the table, his hands behind his back. His eyes narrowed. 'We used not to have all these girls visiting us', he said, 'is it you who attract them?'

Then Ginia lowered her head, but she could tell by his tone of voice that he was not angry. 'Come in', they said, 'don't be silly!'

That afternoon was the best Ginia had ever spent. Her sole fear was that Amelia should turn up and speak her mind. But the time went on, and Guido and Rodrigues kept arguing and every now and then Guido smiled and told her she ought to tell Rodrigues he was an idiot, too. The argument was about pictures, and Guido spoke excitedly and said that colours were colours, after all. Rodrigues, still clasping his knee, faltered and lapsed into silence sometimes, at others he cackled wickedly like a young cockerel. She could not follow Guido's theme but it was a pleasure to listen to him whatever he had to say. He spoke with vehemence and as she gazed at him, she held her breath.

On the roofs, outside, the last rays of the sun were gilding the roof-tops and Ginia from her seat by the window, turned her eyes from the sky to the two men and saw behind in the background the red curtain, and thought how pleasant it would be to be snugly ensconced there, spying on someone who thought he was alone in the room. Just then Guido said, 'It's cold. Is there any tea left?'

'There's tea and a kitchen stove. All that's missing is the cakes'.

'Ginetta will prepare it today', said Guido, turning towards her. 'The stove is behind the curtain'.

'It would be a better idea if she went and bought the cakes', said Rodrigues.

'Nothing doing', replied Ginia, 'It's your place to go, you're a man'.

While the conversation continued, Ginia hunted for the spirit-stove, tea-cups and caddy behind the curtain. She put the water on to boil, rinsed out the cups in the sink there in the dark, curtained off space which the tiny flame did little to brighten. She could hear both their voices at her back; in that corner it was like being in an empty house surrounded by a great peace in which to collect her thoughts. She could only just make out the ruffled bed in that narrow passage between the wall and the curtain. Ginia pictured Amelia lying there.

When she came out, she noticed they were looking at her inquisitively. Ginia had removed her hat by this time, and having glanced behind her, picked up a large plate by the window, all daubed with colours like a palette. But Guido quickly noticed, looked among the packing-cases and handed her a clean one. Ginia stood the cups, which were still damp, on it, returned to the stove and prepared the tea.

As they were drinking it, Guido told her that these cups

were a present from a girl like her who had come to him to have her portrait painted. 'And where is the portrait?' asked Ginia. 'It was not a model', said Guido laughing. 'Shall you be a soldier much longer?' Ginia said, as she calmly sipped her tea.

'To Rodrigues' regret I shall be free in a month's time', Guido replied. He then added, 'You're not offended any more then?'

Ginia could hardly form her lips into a smile and shake her head quickly enough.

'Cut out the formalities in that case!' said Guido.

After supper, particularly, it was wonderful. Amelia, who called to take her home, was very happy too. 'When there's a *festa* and people are idle', she said, 'I'm always happy. Let's take a stroll and have a good laugh together like a couple of fools. Where have you been today?' she asked Ginia as they walked along. 'Nowhere special', Ginia replied. 'Shall we go to the hills and dance?' 'No; summer's over now; it's too muddy up there'. They seemed to find themselves on the way to the studio as if by magic. 'I'm not going there', said Ginia, 'I've had enough of your painters'. 'And who suggested we were going up there? We won't tie ourselves up this evening'. They arrived at the bridge and stopped to admire the pattern of reflections in the water. 'I've seen Barbeta; he asked me about you', remarked Amelia.

'Isn't he tired of drawing you?'

'I saw him at the café'.

'Isn't he giving me the sketch-portraits?'

But while Amelia looked at her, Ginia was thinking about something altogether different.

'What were you doing last year when you used to go to Guido's?'

'What do you think? Having a good laugh and smashing up glasses'.

'So you quarrelled then'.

47

'Need you ask? One summer he went off into the country and no one had as much as a glimpse of him'.

'How did you first get to know him?'

'Why should I remember? Am I an artist's model or not!'

But that evening it was impossible to quarrel and it was too cold to stand still by the water. Amelia had lit her cigarette and was smoking, leaning against the stone parapet.

'Do you smoke in the street as well?' asked Ginia.

'Is it any different from in the café?' retorted Amelia.

But they did not go and sit in a café because Amelia was already fed up with standing all day. They retraced their steps homewards instead, and stopped in front of the cinema. It was too late to go in. While they were examining the display of photographs outside, Severino emerged, looking sullen and annoyed. He raised his chin, acknowledging Amelia, then turned back and began to chat with them. Ginia had never known him so gallant. He at last gave his opinion of Amelia's veil and was amusing about the film. Amelia laughed but in a different way from when she laughed in the café if the waiters made some remark; this time it was with her lips parted, show-ing her teeth, as she used to when in company with her girl friends, but had not done now for some time past. Her voice was certainly hoarse; 'it must be smoking that does it', thought Ginia. Severino accompanied them to the counter and paid for their coffees and told Amelia that they would have to plan a Sunday together. 'Dancing?' 'Rather!' 'Ginia can come along too then', said Amelia. Ginia could not help laughing.

They went with Amelia as far as the door and when it was shut, they went back home. 'Guido is about the same age as Severino', thought Ginia, 'he could be my brother'. 'Life's a rum business', she reflected, 'Guido, who doesn't know him, would take my arm and we would stop at the street-corners and he would tell me that I am a lady, and we would gaze at each other. To him I am Ginetta. We don't need to know each other to be friendly'. And as she pondered, she trotted along by Severino, feeling as if she were still a child. Suddenly she asked him if he was fond of Amelia and realized she had taken him by surprise.

'What does she do in the daytime?' Severino replied.

'She is a model'.

Severino had not understood because he began to tell her that she wore her clothes well, and then Ginia changed the subject and asked him if it was midnight yet.

'You be careful', Severino warned her, 'Amelia is pretty smart; you're just the stooge'.

Ginia told him that they did not often meet and Severino said no more; then he lit a cigarette as he walked along, and they arrived at their door as if they were nothing to do with each other.

Ginia slept little that night; the bed-clothes seemed a dead weight on her. But her mind ran on many things that became more and more fantastic as the time passed by. She imagined herself alone in the unmade bed in that corner of the studio, listening to Guido moving about on the other side of the curtain, living with him, kissing him and cooking for him. She had no idea where Guido had his meals when he was not in the army. Then she began to think that she had never thought of taking up with a soldier but that Guido would make a very handsome civilian, strong and with that blond hair of his; she tried to remember his voice which she had forgotten though she could recall Rodrigues' quite clearly. She must see him again if only to hear him speak. Then as she reflected, she found it difficult to understand why Amelia had fallen for Rodrigues and not for him. She was glad she did not know what Amelia and Guido had done together in the days when they smashed glasses. Just then the alarm went off; she was awake already, thinking of so many things in the warm cosiness of her bed. As dawn broke she regretted that it was now winter and you could not see the lovely colours that accompanied the sun. She wondered if Guido, who said that all colours were really one, was thinking the same thought. 'How lovely', said Ginia to herself and got up.

Nine

Next day, at noon, Amelia called on her, but as Severino was having a meal with her, they only chatted generalities. When they were out in the street, Amelia told her that she had been to a woman-painter that morning who had given her some work. Why didn't she come too. This fool of an artist wanted to do a painting of two women embracing, so they could pose together. 'Why couldn't she copy herself in the mirror?' replied Ginia. 'Do you expect her to take her clothes off to paint?' retorted Amelia, laughing.

Ginia said she could not leave the shop any time she chose. 'But this woman will pay us, you realize that?' said Amelia. 'It's a picture that will take some time to do. If you don't come, she won't take me either'.

'Won't you do alone?'

'There have got to be two women having a scrap, get it? There must be two. It is a large picture. We should only have to pose as if we were dancing together'.

'But I don't want to pose', said Ginia.

'What are you frightened of? She is a woman too, you know'.

'I don't want to'.

They argued as far as the tram and Amelia asked her what she thought she had under her clothes to preserve like a holy of holies. She was in a temper and did not look at her. Ginia did not reply, but when Amelia told her that she would have agreed to take off her clothes for Barbetta, she laughed in her face. They parted on such bad terms that she was doubtful whether Amelia would ever forgive her. But Ginia who at first dismissed the matter with a shrug of her shoulders, suddenly panicked at

51

the thought that Amelia might make her look a fool in front of Guido and Rodrigues, and she was not too confident that Guido would be ingenuous enough not to laugh at her as well. 'I would not mind posing for him', she thought. But she knew very well that Amelia was a better figure than she was and that a painter would prefer her. Amelia was a fully developed woman.

At a late hour she called at the studio for a moment to fore-stall Amelia. It was the time when Guido said he always went along. She found the door locked. It occurred to her that Guido would be at the café with the other two. She passed by the café and looked in the window for a moment but she could only see Amelia sitting there, smoking, with her chin resting on her fist. 'Poor blighter', she thought as she went back home.

After supper she saw from the street that there was a light in the studio and ran upstairs, overjoyed. But Guido was not in. Rodrigues opened the door and let her in and asked her to excuse him because he was terribly hungry and in the middle of a meal. He was standing up by the table, eating salami out of the wrapping; the light was as dim as on the previous occasion. He ate rapaciously, like a boy, digging his teeth into the bread, and if she had not been put off by his swarthy complexion and his shifty eyes, Ginia would have laughed at him. He asked her if she wanted any, but Ginia merely enquired about Guido.

'When he doesn't turn up, it means he's not allowed out', replied Rodrigues. 'He'll be on duty at the barracks'.

'Then I will be off', thought Ginia but dare not say so aloud because he was staring at her and would have realized that Guido was the sole reason for her visit. Undecided, she glanced round the room, which looked almost squalid in that depressing light, with old paper wrappings and cigarette-ends littering the floor, and she asked Rodrigues whether he was expecting anyone.

'Yes', said Rodrigues and stopped chewing.

Not even then could Ginia bring herself to go. She asked him if he had seen Amelia.

'You people do nothing but chase each other round', said Rodrigues, looking at her, 'why, if you are both women?'

'Why?' repeated Ginia.

Rodrigues sighed. 'Why? *You* should know. By intuition. Isn't that how women go on?'

Then Ginia writhed for a second, turning it off with, 'Has Amelia been looking for me?' 'More than that', said Rodrigues, 'she wants you'.

The curtain divided at the back of the studio and Amelia came rushing forward eagerly and Rodrigues, snatching a bite, scuttled round the table as if they were having a game of 'he'. Amelia had not got her hat on and though she seemed put out, stopped in the middle of the room and gave a laugh; but it was an unconvincing one. 'We didn't know you were here', she said.

'Oh, you were having supper', said Ginia curtly.

'An intimate supper', said Rodrigues, 'but it will be more intimate with the three of us'.

'You were looking for Guido, I expect', said Amelia.

'I was just calling, but Rosa is waiting for me. I'm late already'.

Amelia shouted, 'Stop, little idiot!' but Ginia replied, 'I'm not an idiot', and bolted down the stairs.

She thought she was alone when she turned the corner, but she heard someone running after her. It was Amelia, still hatless. 'Why are you rushing off like this? Didn't you believe Rodrigues?'

Without stopping, Ginia shouted, 'Leave me alone!'

She passed several days in this breathless state as if she was still running away. Whenever she thought of those two in the studio, she clenched her fists. She dared not think of Guido and did not know how to set about seeing him. She was convinced she had lost him as well.

'I am a little idiot', she concluded, 'why do I always run away? I still have to learn to be alone. If they want me, they can come and fetch me'.

After that day she felt more at peace and thought of Guido without getting excited, and she began to take some notice of Severino, who whenever they asked him anything, dropped his head before replying and invariably disagreed with whoever had spoken; as often as not he did not reply at all. He was not such a fool, for all he was a man. She, on the other hand, had behaved like Rosa. No wonder people treated her like Rosa.

She gave up going to meet anyone at the cinema or at the dance-hall. She was content to walk in the streets all by herself and pay an occasional visit to the centre of the town. It was November and some evenings she took the tram, got down by the porticoes, strolled round for a short while and then returned home. She always cherished a hope of meeting Guido and glanced cursorily at every soldier as he went by. Chiefly out of curiosity she ventured as far as the café window on one occasion, her heart beating fast; she could vaguely see a number of people but Amelia was not among them.

The days passed by slowly but the cold helped to keep her indoors and Ginia reflected, in the middle of her depression, that there would never be such a summer again. 'I was a different woman then', she thought. 'Can I really have been so crazy? I've come through by a miracle'. It seemed incredible to her that summer would come round another year. And she could already see herself walking down the avenues in the evening, with sore eyes, going from home to work and back home again in the warm air, like a woman of thirty. The worst of it was that she had lost her former partiality for having her little siesta after lunch with the shutters closed. Even when she was busy in the kitchen she thought of the studio and she always had time to do some day-dreaming.

She realized afterwards that she had passed as much as a fortnight like this. She always hoped, on leaving the dressmaker's that she might have some surprise waiting at her door and the fact that no one ever turned up gave the sense of having wasted a day, of being already caught up in the following day or the day after that and of eternally waiting for something that never happened. 'I am not yet seventeen', she thought, 'I have plenty of time before me'. But she could not make out why Amelia, who had run after her hatless, was no more to be seen. Perhaps she was merely afraid she would talk.

One afternoon Signora Bice told her she was wanted on the phone. 'It's a woman with a voice like a man', she added. It was Amelia. 'Listen Ginia, say that Severino is ill and come along to our place. Guido is here too. We will have supper together'. 'But what about Severino?' 'Dash home and knock something up for him and then come here. We will expect you'.

Ginia obeyed and ran home and told Severino she was having supper with Amelia; she tidied her hair. It was raining when she went out. 'Amelia has the voice of a consumptive, poor wretch', she thought.

She had made up her mind to clear off if Guido was not there. She found Amelia and Rodrigues lighting a spirit-stove in the semi-darkness. 'Where's Guido?', she asked. Amelia straightened herself and passing the back of her hand across her brow, pointed to the curtain. From behind it emerged Guido's head. He called out, 'Hello!' and Ginia smiled at him. The table was an untidy mess of paper doylies and food. At that moment a circular reflection from the stove appeared on the ceiling. 'Light the lamp', shouted Guido. 'No, it is nice like this', said Amelia.

It was by no means warm and you needed to keep your overcoat on. Ginia went to the sink, drawing back the curtain and called out from there, 'Whose birthday is it, this evening?' 'Yours if you like', replied Guido softly, drying his hands.

'Why haven't you been coming lately?' 'I came and you weren't in', whispered Ginia, 'Have you been confined to barracks?'

But Guido only smoothed her hair with his fingers.

Just then the light came on behind them and Ginia dropped the curtain and gazed at the still-life of the melon.

They waited until the space round them had got a little warmed up before they began the meal. Strolling about like this with her hands in her coat pocket was like being in the café. Rodrigues poured her out a drink and replenished the other glasses. 'Don't begin', said Amelia. Rodrigues insisted they should. They carefully moved the table over to the sofa so as not to spill the contents of the glasses, and Ginia hurried across to sit next to Amelia on the sofa.

There was salami, fresh fruit, cakes and a couple of bottles of wine. Ginia wondered if this was the sort of party Amelia used to have with Guido, and when she had drunk a glass of wine, asked him point-blank, and then the two of them proceeded to laugh and remind each other of all the funny things they had done behind there. Ginia listened jealously – she seemed to have been born too late and felt a fool. It occurred to her that artists are a joke because their lives are different from other people's; even Rodrigues, who did not paint, lapsed into silence and chewed away or, if he did air his views, did so in a jeering way. She took it all in, quietly hostile, angry because Guido had fooled round with Amelia.

'It is not very nice', she complained, 'telling me all these things when I wasn't there'.

'But you're here now', said Amelia, 'enjoy yourself!'

Then Ginia felt a terrible desire to be all alone with Guido. Yet she knew that it was only Amelia's presence that was giving her the necessary courage. Otherwise she would have run off. 'I don't seem to have learnt to keep quiet', she repeated to herself, 'I ought not to get worked up'.

Then the others lit their cigarettes and offered her one. Ginia did not really want it but Guido came and sat beside her and lit it for her, telling her not to inhale. The other two were engaged in an amorous tussle on a corner of the sofa.

Then Ginia leapt to her feet, pushed Guido's hands away, put down her cigarette and walked across the studio without speaking. She moved the curtain aside and stood still in the darkness. The conversation behind her sounded like a distant buzz. 'Guido', she whispered, without looking round, and threw herself, face downwards, on the bed.

Ten

All four of them left the place in silence, Guido and Rodrigues accompanying them as far as the tram. Guido with his beret pulled over his eyes looked quite different, but he pressed her hands in his and said, 'darling Ginetta'. As they strolled along, the pavement seemed to be rocking under her feet. Amelia took her arm.

While they were waiting for the tram, they began talking about bicycles, but Guido came close to her and said in a gentle voice, 'Mind you don't change your mind. I would never do your portrait if you did'. Ginia smiled and took his hand.

When they had boarded the tram, Ginia stood staring at the driver's back and fell silent. 'Go home and put yourself to bed', said Amelia, 'it's the result of the wine more than anything else'. 'I'm not drunk', said Ginia, 'don't you believe me?' 'Would you like me to see you home?' said Amelia. 'Leave me alone, for Heaven's sake'. Then Amelia spoke to her about the other occasion, explaining how it had been, and Ginia just listened to the noise of the tram.

When she was alone, she began to feel better because there was no one looking at her. She sat on the edge of the bed and stayed there for an hour staring at the floor. Then she suddenly got undressed, flung herself down and put out the light.

The next day was sunny, and as Ginia got dressed she felt as if she had been ill. She thought that Guido would have been up three hours already, and she smiled into the mirror and threw herself a kiss. Then she went out before Severino should return.

It seemed futile walking along in the usual way, being hungry, for her mind was fixed only on one thing, that from now on she must have Guido to herself without the other two. But Guido had invited her to the studio, he had not said a word about meeting her outside. 'I need to be very fond of him', thought Ginia. 'I'd feel let down otherwise'. The summer had suddenly returned and with it the desire to go out, laugh and have a good time. She could not believe that what had happened was really true. She found herself laughing at the thought that in the dark Guido would have behaved in the same way if she had been Amelia. 'It is obvious he likes the way I talk, look and how I am. He likes me as a sweetheart; he loves me. He did not believe I was seventeen, but he kissed my eyes; I am a grown-up woman now'.

How pleasant it was to walk along all day, thinking of the studio and waiting for evening. 'I am more than a model', said Ginia, 'we are friends'. She was sorry for Amelia because she did not understand the beauty in Guido's pictures. But at two o'clock when she came to pick her up, Ginia wanted to ask her something but did not know how to begin. She had not the nerve to ask Guido.

'Have you seen anyone?'

Amelia shrugged her shoulders.

'Yesterday when you put out the light, my head seemed to be going round. I think I cried out. Did you hear me?'

Amelia was listening attentively. 'It wasn't me putting out the light', she replied gently, 'all I noticed was that you had disappeared. I thought Guido must be murdering you. I hope you enjoyed yourselves at any rate'.

Ginia frowned and looked straight in front of her. They walked on to the next tram-stop.

'Do you like Rodrigues?' asked Ginia.

Amelia sighed and said, 'Don't worry your head. I don't care for blond men, if anything I prefer blonde women'.

Then Ginia's face softened into a smile and she said no more. She was quite happy to walk along with Amelia and feel they were on such friendly terms. They parted company under the porticoes, without fuss, and Ginia watched her from the corner where she stood, for a minute wondering whether she was going to pose at that woman-painter's.

Meantime she herself went back to the studio at seven o'clock and climbed up five floors without hurrying so as not to get red in the face. Without hurrying, but two steps at a time. All the while she thought that even if Guido was not in, it was not his fault. But the door was open. Guido had heard her walking along the corridor and had come to meet her. Ginia was now in her seventh heaven.

She wanted to talk and tell him all manner of things but Guido closed the door and the first thing he did was to hug her. A little daylight still fell from the windows, and Ginia buried her face on his shoulders. She could feel his warm flesh through his shirt. They sat down on the sofa without saying anything and Ginia began to weep. As she wept, she thought, 'supposing Guido were to cry, too', and a burning sensation ran through her whole body as if she was going to faint. Suddenly the support was removed; she realized that Guido was getting up and she opened her eyes. Guido was standing there looking at her, puzzled. She stopped crying then because she felt as if she was crying in public. As he looked at her Ginia who could hardly see, felt more tears welling into her eyes. 'Steady on', said Guido light-heartedly, 'if there's so little to come into this world for, it's hardly worth crying over'. 'I am crying because I am so happy', said Ginia softly. 'That's all right then', said Guido, 'but let's know at once another time!' So that half-hour, when Ginia would have liked to ask him lots of things about Amelia, about himself, his pictures, what he did in the evenings and if he loved her, she could not screw up the necessary courage. She managed to get him to go behind the curtain, however; in the light she somehow felt in full view of everybody. While they were kissing there, Ginia quietly told him he had made her cry out yesterday, and Guido's manner then became more gentle; he cheered her up, renewed his caresses and whispered in her ear, 'You see what's happening; I'm not hurting you, am I?' Then while they lay back in the cosy warmth, he explained all kinds of things to her, telling her he respected a girl of her sort and that she could trust him. Then Ginia squeezed his hand in the dark and kissed it.

Now she knew that Guido was so good, she became bolder and with her head leaning against his shoulder, told him she had always wanted to have him to herself because she felt fine with him but not with the others there. 'In the evening Rodrigues comes back here to sleep', said Guido, 'I can't put him out on the tiles. We work here you know!' But Ginia told him that she would be content with an hour, even a few minutes, that *she* worked too and had dashed away from the shop every evening at that time in the hope of finding him alone. 'When you're in civilian life again, will you still see Rodrigues?' she asked him. 'I should so like to see you paint when no one else is there'. Then she told him she would sit for him, only if he would agree to that. As they lay stretched there in the darkness, Ginia did not notice that night was coming on.

That night Severino had to go to work on an empty stomach but it was not the first time, and he never complained. Ginia did not leave the studio until Rodrigues arrived.

Guido spent the last days before his demobilisation priming and drying his canvases, adjusting his easel and generally tidying the studio. He never went out. It seemed a foregone conclusion that Rodrigues would continue to live there with him. But Rodrigues always messed everything up and whenever Ginia was in a hurry, started up a conversation. Ginia would have been only too happy to help Guido clean and tidy up the studio, but a glance at Rodrigues told her that it would have annoyed them, and she went back to go out with Amelia. They joined forces and went to the cinema because each of them was holding something back from the other and they would have found an evening's chat hard going.

It was clear that Amelia had something on her mind; she was railing against all blonds, male and female. But at the moment Ginia felt kindly disposed towards her and was unable to hide her thoughts. As they walked back home, she brought them out.

She asked her if she had come to any arrangement with the woman-artist. Amelia put on a puzzled look and told her she had let it go. 'No', said Ginia, 'what a thing to do; I know I've never sat but I'm sorry you have lost the job'. 'Don't mention it', said Amelia, 'you've found love these last days, you can snap your fingers at everyone else. Why not! – but if I were you. I'd watch my step'.

'Why?' asked Ginia.

'What has Severino got to say? Does he approve of your friend?' said Amelia with a laugh.

'Why ought I to watch my step?' asked Ginia.

'You take away my best painter and then you ask?'

Then Ginia's heart began to thump and she felt Amelia's eyes boring into her as she walked along.

'Have you ever posed for Guido?' she asked.

Amelia took her by the arm and said, 'I was only joking'.

Then, after a pause, 'No, it's much more pleasant for us two who are women and know it, to go out for a walk together than demean ourselves mixing with unscrupulous oafs whose only idea about girls is to make a bee-line for the first one they clap eyes on'.

'But you go out with Rodrigues', said Ginia.

Amelia merely shrugged her shoulders and made an exclamation of disgust, adding, 'Tell me one thing, is Guido careful, anyhow?'

'I don't know what you mean', said Ginia.

Amelia took her by the chin and forced her to stop. 'Look me in the face', she said. They were in the shadow of a porch. Ginia offered no resistance because it was all to do with Guido, and Amelia kissed her swiftly on the lips.

Eleven

They walked on again and Ginia gave a frightened smile under Amelia's stares. 'Powder your face', said Amelia in quiet tones. Ginia, without stopping, looked at herself in her mirror until she reached the next lamp and did not dare leave off, examining her eyes and tidying her hair as well. 'I may as well tell you – I have been drinking tonight', said Amelia when they had gone past the lamp-post. Ginia replaced her mirror and continued to walk on without replying. Their steps rang out on the pavement. When they reached the street-corner, Amelia hesitated. Ginia said, 'Well, here we are'. They turned and when they reached the door, Amelia said 'Cheerio'. 'Cheerio', said Ginia, and continued on her way.

Next day Guido lit the light when she entered because there was a fog outside and it seemed to have found its way in through the huge windows. 'Why don't you light the stove?' she asked him. 'It is lit', said Guido, who was wearing his jacket this time, 'don't worry, we'll light the fire this winter'. Ginia walked round the room, raised a piece of material nailed to the wall and discovered a tiny room full of rubbish and piles of books. 'What a nice room! Is this where you put your sitter?' 'If it's in the nude', said Guido. Then they dragged a suitcase from under the bed behind the curtain; it contained Guido's wardrobe. 'You've had models then?' asked Ginia. 'Let's see the portfolios of drawings'.

Guido took her by the arm. 'What a lot you know about painters. Tell me, do you know any?' Ginia laughed, put her finger to her lips and struggled to get away. 'Come on, show me the portfolios. You told Amelia lots of girls came here'.

'Naturally', said Guido, 'it's my job'. Then to hold her there, he kissed her. 'Which artist do you know?'

'I don't know any', said Ginia, throwing her arms round him. 'You are the only one I want to know and I don't want anyone else ever to come here'. 'We'd get bored', said Guido.

That evening Ginia wanted to sweep the room but there was no broom to do it and she had to content herself with remaking the bed behind the curtain, where it was as ill-kept as an animal's den. 'Will you be sleeping here?' she asked. Guido said that he liked to be able to see the windows at night and would sleep on the sofa. 'I won't make the bed then', said Ginia.

She arrived the following day carrying a parcel in her handbag. It was a tie for Guido. He took it laughingly and held it against his grey-green shirt. 'It will look nice with your civvies', said Ginia. Then they went behind the curtain and lay on the unmade bed in each other's arms, drawing the coverlet over them because it was chilly. Guido told her that it was he who ought to be giving her presents and Ginia made a grimace and asked him for a broom to sweep out the studio.

The days when they had these brief times together were the best, but they could never have a leisurely chat because Rodrigues might turn up at any moment and Ginia did not want to be discovered with her shoes off. But one of the last of these evenings, Guido said he wanted to pay back his debts, and they arranged to go out after supper. 'Let's go to the cinema', said Guido. 'Why? let's have a walk instead, it is so nice just to be together'. 'But it's cold', said Guido. 'What about going to a café or a dance-hall'. 'I don't like dancing', said Guido.

So they met and Ginia felt impressed to be walking next to a sergeant, then she thought it was Guido and no one else. Guido held her under the armpit as if she were a child. But he kept having to salute officers and then Ginia transferred herself to the other side and hung on to his arm. As they walked along like this, the street seemed somehow different.

'Supposing we meet Amelia', thought Ginia and began talking about Signora Bice, trying not to laugh. Guido was in a joking mood too and said, 'In three days' time I shan't have to be saluting these monkeys. Look at their miserable shopkeepers' faces'. 'Amelia liked stopping to jeer at passers-by, too', said Ginia.

'Amelia goes a bit too far sometimes. Have you known her long then?'

'We're neighbours', said Ginia, 'have you?'

Then Guido told her about the year when he had rented the studio and his student friends came to look him up, and there had been one who had become a monk. Amelia was not a professional model then, but she had been fond of taking her clothes off and they all used to gather morning and night and laughed and drank together while he tried to work. He could not remember precisely when he had been with Amelia for the first time. Then one of their number had joined the army, another had passed his exams, one of them had got married: the happy days were over.

'Are you sorry?' asked Ginia, staring at him.

'Not as sorry as the monk, who writes to me now and again and asks me if I am working and whether I see anyone'.

'But are they allowed to write?'

'They're not in prison, dammit', said Guido. 'And he was the only one who liked my pictures. You should have seen him; a strong chap like me, tall with eyes like a girl's. He'd got the hang of it; pity'.

'I hope you won't become a monk, Guido'.

'No danger of that'.

'Rodrigues doesn't like your pictures; now *he* does look like a priest'.

But Guido defended Rodrigues and told her he was an extraordinary painter – one of those who thinks deeply before he starts to work and never leaves anything to chance – and that colour was his only trouble. 'There's too much colour in his country', he said. 'He's had his bellyful of it as a kid and now he prefers to dispense with it. But, by Jove, he's clever'.

'Will you let me watch when you paint?' asked Ginia, squeezing his arm.

'If I am still capable of painting when I get rid of this uniform. I used to get some work done before. I used to finish a picture a week. They were exciting, those days, but the good days are over'.

'Don't I matter to you?' asked Ginia.

Then Guido pressed her arm. 'You're not the summer. You don't know what it is to paint a picture. I ought to fall in love with you to teach you all about it. Then I should be wasting time. An artist can only work, you know, if he has friends who understand what he's up to'.

'Haven't you ever been in love?' asked Ginia, avoiding his eyes.

'What, with you folk? I haven't time'.

When they were tired of walking, they adjourned to the café to continue their love-making. Guido lit a cigarette and listened as she chatted away to him, watching the people as they came in and out. Then, to please her, he drew her profile on the marble table-top. When they were alone for a minute Ginia said, 'I'm glad you have never been in love before'.

'I'm glad you're pleased', said Guido.

The evening ended on a rather gloomy note because it turned out that once Guido had said goodbye to the army, he intended going off into the country to see his mother. Ginia consoled herself as well as she could, getting him to talk about his parents and his home, his father's occupation and his boyhood days. She knew he had a sister called Luisa. But she was disappointed really that Guido was a countryman at heart. 'As a boy I went about barefooted', he confessed with a smile, and then Ginia understood the reason for his strong hands and his loud voice and could not believe that a country peasant could paint pictures. The odd thing was that Guido should boast of it and when Ginia said to him, 'But yet you stay here', he replied that the country was where real painting was done. 'Yet you stay here', repeated Ginia. 'But I am only really happy on the top of a hill', was Guido's reply.

From that moment Ginia, for some reason or other, thought frequently about Luisa and envied her her position as Guido's sister and tried to imagine the conversations which Guido might have had with her as a boy. Now she understood why Amelia had never tried to take up with him. 'If he weren't a painter, he would just be an ordinary peasant', and she pictured him as a conscript, one of the lads who go marching by with a handkerchief knotted round their throats, singing, and end up as soldiers. 'But he is here', she reflected, 'he's done his time as a student, and we both have the same coloured hair'. She wondered if Luisa was blonde too. That evening when Ginia had arrived home, she locked the door and then got undressed in front of the mirror and looked at herself, absorbed, comparing her skin with the colour of Guido's neck. Then she felt at ease again and it seemed strange to her that there were no marks left on her. She imagined herself posing before Guido, and she sat down on a chair in the way Amelia had done that day in Barbetta's studio. Heaven knew how many girls Guido had seen. The only one he had not really seen was herself, and Ginia's heart beat fast at the mere thought. How lovely it would be to become dark, slim, devil-may-care like Amelia all of a sudden. But she could not let herself be seen naked by Guido; they must get married first.

But Ginia knew he would never marry her, however fond she was of him. She had known this from that evening when she had offered herself to him. Guido was too good to stop his work to come behind the curtain with her. Only if she became his model could she go on seeing him. Otherwise one fine day he would find another.

Ginia felt chilly there before the mirror and flung her coat over her bare thighs; it gave her goose flesh. 'Look, that's how it would be if I posed', she said, and envied Amelia who had ceased to have any sense of shame.

Twelve

When Ginia had seen Guido the previous time, the evening before he went off to the country, she suddenly felt that making love in the way he wanted it, was a desperate business and she lay there as though benumbed, to such an extent that Guido drew back the curtain to see her face, but Ginia took hold of his hands to try and stop him. Then when Rodrigues arrived and Ginia left them to talk, she understood what it was not to be married and able to spend day and night together. She went downstairs, bewildered, and for the moment she was convinced that she had become somebody different and that they were all ignoring her. 'That is why love-making is frowned on; that must be the reason'. And she wondered whether Amelia and Rosa had called. Seeing her reflection in the shop-windows, reeling as if she was drunk, she felt she bore no relation to that vague image which was moving past like a shadow. She now realized why all actresses have that haggard look in their eyes. But it wasn't that that made you pregnant; actresses did not have babies.

As soon as Severino had gone out, Ginia closed the door and undressed in front of the mirror. She found herself unchanged; she could not believe it. She ran her hand over her skin as if it was something separate from her body which still gave a few final shudders. But she was otherwise no different; she was as white and pale as ever. 'Guido should see me if he were here', she thought hastily, 'I would let him look at me. I would tell him that I really am a woman now'.

Sunday came along, and it was hard having to spend it without Guido there. Amelia came to look her out, and Ginia was pleased because she was no longer in awe of her, and having Guido to occupy her mind, she no longer needed to take her too seriously. She let her chatter away while she herself thought of her secret. Amelia, poor creature, was more alone than she was.

Not even Amelia knew where to suggest going. It was a short, chilly afternoon, damp with fog, which discouraged them from going to the sports ground to see the match. Amelia asked for a drink of coffee; her idea was to lie back on the sofa, talking. But Ginia put her hat on and said, 'Let's go out; I want to go up to the hills'.

Amelia, strangely enough, was quite submissive; she was feeling lazy that day. They took the tram to get there more quickly, though there was no particular hurry. Ginia discoursed, set the pace, chose the route as if she had a definite purpose. It started to drizzle as they began the ascent, and when Amelia grumbled, Ginia refused to show any concern. 'It's only a mountain mist', she said, 'it's nothing'. They were now on the wide, empty road, passing under the trees of the park-enclosures; it was as though they were outside the world altogether, hearing only the gurgling of the roadside stream and the rattle of the trams in the remote distance. They began to inhale the freshly-washed air and became aware of the smell of rotting leaves, more pervasive than the cold. Amelia gradually came to life and they hurried along the asphalt arm in arm, laughing and saying they must be crazy and that not even lovers went to the hills in weather like that.

A luxurious-looking car came along, and, after passing them, slowed down. 'We could have that!' remarked Amelia. A grey clad arm shot out of the car and beckoned to them. 'May I offer you a lift?' said the driver when they were within range. He was sucking a caramel. 'Shall we accept, Amelia?' whispered Ginia, smiling. 'Rather', said Amelia, 'he can take us as far as the Devil's House and then leave us to go on foot'. As they walked on, he followed them at the same rate, making inane remarks and blowing his horn. 'I am going to get in', said Amelia, 'if you don't mind; it's better than wearing your shoes out'. 'Isn't your blonde friend coming?' the man remarked, getting out. He was in his forties and very thin.

They then got in, Amelia in the middle and Ginia crushed against the door. The lean man wormed his way under the steering-wheel and began by putting one arm round Amelia's shoulder. Seeing the dark, bony hand near her ear, Ginia thought, 'If he lays a finger on me, I'll murder him'. But they suddenly started off, and she had a side-view of a face, that bore an ugly scar on the temple, concentrated on the road. Ginia, her cheek pressed against the window, thought how pleasant it would be to spend her time travelling like this all the week Guido was away.

However, her dream came to an abrupt end. The car slowed down at an open space and stopped. The handsome trees had given way to this wilderness filled with mist and telegraph-wires. The hillside looked like a bare mountain. 'Do you want to get out here?' said the man, still sucking his caramel, and turning to them.

Ginia said, 'You go on to the café then, I'll walk back on foot'. Amelia scowled at her. 'She's crazy!' the man exclaimed. 'I'll walk back', Ginia repeated. 'There are two of you and two's company'. 'Stupid!' hissed Amelia as they were getting out of the car, 'don't you see, it's not just talk with this chap; he'll pay'. But Ginia turned her head and called out, 'Thanks for everything. See you bring my friend home safely!'

When she got to the road, she listened a moment in the silence of the fog to hear if the engine had started up again. Then she laughed to herself and began the descent. 'Oh, Guido, they're ruining me', she thought, and looked at the hillsides, sniffing the cold air and the country. Guido too was on the naked earth among his own hills. Perhaps he was at home near the fire, smoking a cigarette as he did in the studio to warm himself up. Then Ginia stopped as the picture rose before her of the warm, dark corner behind the curtain. 'Oh Guido, come back!' she murmured, clenching her fists in her pockets.

She soon got back, but her soaked hair, splashed stockings and her weariness remained to keep her company. She threw off her shoes, stretched herself full length on the warm bed and communed in thought with the absent Guido. She thought of the smart car, sharing Amelia's thrill, and concluding that she must have met the gentleman before.

When Severino returned, she told him she was bored with working at the dressmaker's. 'Have a change then', he said, unmoved, 'but don't make me have to skip any more meals. Find some post with more reasonable hours'.

'There's so many things to do'.

'Mamma used to say you'd enough at home to keep you busy. Considering what you earn outside!'

Ginia leapt up from the sofa. 'We've not paid a visit to the cemetery this year'.

'I have been', stated Severino. 'Don't lie. You know you haven't'.

But Ginia was merely saying something for the sake of talking. Except for her small earnings, she would have nothing to put on her back and would never be able to afford gloves to put on for washing-up and so save her hands. And the scent, the hat, the face-cream, the presents for Guido would be for ever beyond her reach; she would be no better off than a factory-girl like Rosa. What she lacked was time. She needed work that could be disposed of in the mornings.

Moreover a job had its compensations. What would she have done during these days of Guido's absence if she had had to stay at home all day or vaguely wander round, worrying her head off? As it was, she went back to the shop next day, which she got through somehow. She hurried home and prepared a nice supper for Severino and decided to compensate during these next days for the meals that she had failed more than once to cook for him.

Amelia did not appear. Several evenings Ginia was on the point of going out when she remembered her private vow to stay in, and she hoped Amelia would call. Rosa came once. She wanted to make herself a coat and show her the pattern. But Ginia found it hard to make conversation. They discussed Pino, but Rosa did not confess that she had changed him for someone else. She complained instead that she was bored to death and said, 'What do you expect? If you get married, you're landed'.

Ginia realized that continually thinking about Guido was interfering with her sleep, and sometimes she got angry because he failed to understand that he ought to come back. 'I wonder if he will be here by Monday', she thought, 'I am sure he's not coming'. She particularly hated Luisa, who was only his sister, and yet had the pleasure of seeing him all day long. She was overcome by such nostalgia that she considered going along to his studio and finding out from Rodrigues if Guido was keeping his word.

But she went to the café instead and saw Amelia. 'How did it go on Sunday?' she asked. Amelia, who was smoking a cigarette, did not even smile, and said quietly, 'It went fine'. 'Did he take you home?' 'Yes indeed', said Amelia.

Then she asked, 'Why did you run off?'

'Wasn't he offended?'

'What rot', said Amelia, staring at her. 'All he said was: "Spirited little piece". Why *did* you run off?'

Ginia felt herself blush. 'I thought he looked ridiculous with that caramel'.

'You're a fool', said Amelia.

'What news of Rodrigues?'

'He is away at present'.

They walked back home together and Amelia said to her, 'Tonight I'll come and see you'.

There was no talk of going out that evening. Ginia, having got the washing-up out of the way, sat down on the edge of the sofa, where Amelia was lying at full length. They remained thus for a while in silence, and then Amelia whispered in her husky voice, 'Spirited little piece!' Ginia shook her head and looked away. Amelia stretched her arm out and stroked her hair. 'Leave me alone', said Ginia.

With a great sigh, Amelia raised herself up on her elbow. 'I dote on you', she said huskily. Ginia darted a look at her. 'But I can't kiss you. I've got syphilis'.

Thirteen

'Do you know what it is?'

Ginia's eyes expressed silent assent.

'But I didn't myself'.

'Who told you, then?'

'Haven't you noticed how I talk?' said Amelia, in a choky voice.

'That's from smoking'.

'That's what I thought', said Amelia, 'But our fine friend of last Sunday was a doctor. Look!' She opened her blouse and showed one of her breasts. Ginia said, 'I don't believe you'.

Amelia raised her eyes, holding it between her fingers, and looked at her. 'All right, kiss me here then!' she said quietly, 'where it is inflamed'. They stared at each other for a moment; then Ginia closed her eyes and bent forward over her breast.

'Oh no!' exclaimed Amelia, 'I've already given you a kiss'.

Ginia felt herself growing hot all over — she gave a stupid smile and blushed a fiery red. Amelia looked at her without saying a word. 'I see you're a fool', she said finally, 'you're being nice to me just now while you're in love with Guido and I don't matter to you any more'.

Ginia was puzzled what to answer because she herself did not know what she should have done. But she did not mind Amelia's criticism, because she now knew what nudes and poses were and understood her jargon. She allowed Amelia to go on talking excitedly but at the same time she was conscious of a nausea like that she had felt as a child when she was having a bath and was undressing on a chair close to the stove.

But when Amelia said that the disease was carried in the bloodstream, Ginia was frightened.

'What do they do?' she asked.

Amelia told her it was hopeless unless you took things quietly, and that they would take a specimen of blood from her arm with a syringe. She said they made them strip and kept them standing in the cold for more than half an hour. The doctor was always in a bad temper and threatened to pack her off to the hospital.

'He can't', said Ginia.

'What a kid you are!' said Amelia. 'They could send me to prison if they had a mind to. You don't know what syphilis is'.

'But where did you get it?'

Amelia looked at her evasively. 'You get it love-making'.

'But one of the two must have it first'. 'Quite', replied Amelia.

Then Ginia remembered about Guido and felt so faint she could not speak.

Amelia had sat down and was supporting her breast under her blouse with her hand. She stared round vaguely; in her present state, without her veil and in utter dejection, there was no wonder she was no longer herself. At intervals she clenched her teeth, baring her gums. Not even the perfume she had on could soothe her.

'You ought to have seen Rodrigues', she said all at once in her hoarse voice, 'it was he who said you go blind and die of ulcers. He turned white right down to his neck'. Amelia made a face as if she were spitting. 'It always happens like that. He is all right'.

Ginia asked her in such haste whether she was really certain that Amelia hesitated. 'No, you've no need to worry; they've made a blood test on him. Are you afraid for Guido?'

Ginia forced a smile and lowered her eyes. Amelia kept quiet for what seemed an eternity, then she suddenly snapped out, 'Guido has never touched me, don't worry!'

Then Ginia cheered up; so much so that she put her hand on Amelia's shoulder. Amelia frowned. 'Aren't you afraid of touching me?' she said. 'But we're not love-making', stammered Ginia.

Her heart did not cease pounding all the time Amelia was speaking of Guido. She told her that she had not even kissed Guido because one can't make love with everybody and, though she liked him, she could not understand why Ginia should find him attractive when they were both blonds. Ginia felt herself go hot all over again and was thoroughly happy.

'But if Rodrigues hasn't got it', she said, 'it means you haven't either. They've made a mistake'.

Amelia looked at her rather shiftily. 'What's your idea? Were you thinking he had given it to me?'

'I don't know', said Ginia.

'If he's afraid that a child . . .' began Amelia between her teeth. 'But not he. The Lord chasteneth. The woman who gave me the present is worse than me. She doesn't know it yet; it appears she may go blind'.

'It's a woman then!' whispered Ginia.

'Has been for more than two months. This mark is a present from her', and she tapped her blouse. Ginia tried to console her all the evening but was careful not to come into close contact with her, and took comfort as she remembered they had never done more than go arm in arm, and that Amelia had said furthermore that you could not catch it unless you had an open wound because it was a blood-infection. Ginia was convinced, but she dare not express her thought, that these things followed in the wake of the kind of sins that Amelia committed. Then she tried not to think about it, for in that case they ought all of them to be sick people.

However, as they went downstairs, she told her she ought not to feel vindictive towards the woman in question; if she did not know, she could not be to blame. But Amelia stopped on the stair and interrupted, 'Shall I send her a bouquet then?'

They made a rendezvous for the next day at the café and Ginia watched her walk off into the distance, deeply stirred.

Ginia could hardly bear with herself next day. She left the house an hour before the lamps were lit and hurried to the studio. She did not dare go up straight away because Rodrigues was asleep, and paced about in the cold underneath until she thought she heard him turn over in bed. Then she ran up, trembling all over, and knocked at the door.

She found Rodrigues in his pyjamas looking at her with sleepy eyes. After stalking round the room, he sat down on the edge of the bed. There was dirt everywhere, the light was as glaring as usual. Ginia began in a stammering voice and Rodrigues sat there scratching his legs until she asked him if he had been to the doctor's. Then they both let go about Amelia, and Ginia noticed there was a tremor in her voice. She averted her gaze from his ugly feet.

Rodrigues said, 'I'm going back to bed; it's damn cold', and he went back, drawing the bed-cover round him.

When Ginia, still trembling, told him she had been kissed by Amelia, he began to laugh, lying there propped up on his elbow in the semi-darkness. 'We're colleagues then', he said. 'Only a kiss?'

'Yes', said Ginia, 'is there any danger?'

'What sort of kiss?'

Ginia did not understand. He explained what he meant and Ginia swore that it had been just a kiss between one girl and another.

'Innocent fun', remarked Rodrigues, 'don't you worry'.

Ginia was standing up in front of the curtain and on the table was a dirty glass and some orange-peel. 'When does Guido come back?' she asked.

'Monday', said Rodrigues. 'See that? It's a still-life'. He pointed to the glass.

Ginia smiled and moved to the side. 'Sit down, Ginia, here on the bed'.

'I must run', she replied, 'I've got to work'.

But Rodrigues complained that she had woken him up and now she wouldn't even stay to exchange the time of day, 'To celebrate our escape from danger', he added.

Ginia sat on the edge of the bed by the drawn curtain. 'I'm worried about Amelia', she said. 'Poor creature. She's desperate. Do you really go blind?'

'Of course not', said Rodrigues, 'you get cured. They bore lots of holes in her and will remove some bits of skin and before long the doctor friend will be taking her to bed, you'll see'.

Ginia tried not to smile and Rodrigues continued, 'Did he take both of you up to the hills?' As he spoke he stroked her hands as if they had been a cat's back.

'What frozen hands', he said. 'Why don't you come and warm them?'

Ginia allowed herself to be kissed on the neck, saying 'Be good!' Then she rose to her feet, blushing, and dashed out.

Fourteen

That evening Rodrigues came to the café too and sat down at the next table, over by Ginia.

'How's the voice?' he asked half joking.

Ginia was trying to comfort Amelia, explaining to her how one got better, and sat there quiet and contented. They hardly exchanged a glance with Rodrigues.

Amelia sat there quietly, too. She was thinking of asking the time when Rodrigues said sarcastically, 'Bravo! so we're seducing minors now, are we?'

Amelia did not grasp the illusion at once and Ginia quickly shut her eyes. By the time she had opened them, she heard Amelia saying fiercely, 'What has this idiot been telling you?'

But Rodrigues spared her. He just said, 'She came to wake me up this morning to hear about you from me'.

'He enjoys himself', said Amelia.

During the next days Ginia endeavoured to be on her best behaviour because Guido was really coming back, and she went to look up Rodrigues. Not at the studio any longer; it was rather a frightening memory, and, besides, Rodrigues was a long-sleeper, but at the little restaurant where he ate and where Guido doubtless went too. It was in the street on the tram-route and she passed a few moments exchanging pleasantries and to find out if there was anything new. She behaved rather like Amelia and pulled his leg. But Rodrigues now knew where he got off and no longer made passes at her. They arranged between them that she should go along to the studio on the Sunday and do a little cleaning-up ready for Guido's homecoming. 'We syphilitics', said Rodrigues, 'don't give a damn for anything!'

Amelia, however, had ceased going there. Ginia stayed with her on the Saturday afternoon and accompanied her to the doctor who was giving her the injections. They stopped at the door, and finally Amelia said, 'Don't go up; they might find something wrong with you too', and ran up the stairs, with a final 'Cheerio, Ginia', so that Ginia, who had started out quite cheerfully, went home depressed. Not even the thought that Guido would be there within twenty-four hours could comfort her.

Sunday, too, passed like a dream. Ginia remained in the studio all the afternoon, and swept round, polished and generally tidied the place. Rodrigues did not even attempt to get in her way. He even helped her to cart off mountains of waste-paper and fruit-peel. Then they banged the dust out of the books on the mantelpiece and put them on top of a bookcase. While they were in the middle of washing the paint-brushes, Ginia paused a moment, enraptured: the smell of the turps brought back the memory of Guido almost as if he was there. She smiled because Rodrigues could not understand.

'He's a lucky swine', said Rodrigues when Ginia had finished and was emerging from behind the curtain with a duster, 'if he only knew it'.

They then had tea together by the stove and looked through the drawings of Guido's they had found under the books; but Ginia was disappointed because they consisted only of landscapes and one portrait-head of an old man. 'Wait a minute', said Rodrigues, 'I know what you're after'.

And after a while came drawings of women. They looked like fashion-plates. Ginia was amused, for they were dressed in the fashion of two years before. Next came some female nudes; then male nudes, and Ginia hurriedly turned them over because Rodrigues, who had been leaning back against the wall, was now bending forward. Last of all came a drawing of a young woman, fully clothed; she had a squarish face and had the head and shoulders of a peasant. 'Who is it?' asked Ginia.

'It'll be his sister'.

'Luisa?'

'I don't know'.

Ginia studied the large eyes and the subtle mouth. She saw no resemblance to anyone else. 'She's beautiful', she said, 'she's none of that dreamy look that you painters usually give them'. 'Speak for him', replied Rodrigues, 'leave me out of it!'

Ginia was in such a happy frame of mind that, had Rodrigues known it, he might have kissed her, instead of which he lay back on the sofa looking depressed. If it had not been for a little daylight that still stole in through the window, Ginia could have imagined it to be Guido near her and would have caressed him. She shut her eyes to think of him.

'How nice it is here', she said aloud.

Then she asked Rodrigues once again if he knew the exact time of tomorrow's event and he said that Guido would certainly be cycling back. The conversation turned on the villages in Guido's part of the country, and although he had never been to any of them, Rodrigues jokingly described them as being composed of pig-sties and hen-runs and with roads that were so rough at that season of the year that Guido might not be able to get away. Ginia pouted her lips and told him not to tease her.

They went out together and Rodrigues promised not to spill his cigarette-ash about. 'I'll sleep on a bench tonight. How will that be?' They passed through the door smiling, and Ginia boarded the tram, thinking of Amelia and the girls depicted in the drawings, comparing herself with them. It seemed but yesterday that they had gone to the hills and now Guido was coming back.

She woke up next day in a great state of consternation. It was midday before she could turn round. She had agreed with

Rodrigues that if Guido arrived, they would meet at the café. She went past it on tiptoe and caught sight of them at the bar through the window. Guido looked thin in his mackintosh; he was standing there with one foot supported on the metal bar. If he had been alone, Ginia would not have recognized him. His open mackintosh allowed her to see a grey tie; Guido in civilian clothes no longer seemed a young man.

He and Rodrigues were engaged in conversation and laughing. Ginia thought, 'If only Amelia were there, I could pretend I was on my way to her place'. Before she could bring herself to enter, she had to remind herself that she had tidied up the studio.

She was still hovering in the doorway when Guido spotted her. She walked towards him as if she was there by chance. Never before had Guido made her feel so ill at ease. Guido extended his hand to her in the midst of all the customers who were coming and going, and continued to speak with his head turned towards Rodrigues.

They hardly exchanged more than a word. Guido was nervous because of the others watching. He encouraged her with a smile, calling out, 'Are you all right?' and then, by the door, 'Goodbye!'

Ginia walked in the direction of the tram, smiling like an idiot. Suddenly she felt her arm taken and a voice, Guido's, whispered in her ear, 'Ginetta'.

They stopped and Ginia had tears in her eyes. 'Where are you going?' he asked. 'Home'. 'Without welcoming me?' and Guido squeezed her arm and fixed his eyes on her. 'Oh Guido', said Ginia, 'I was just waiting for you'.

They went back on the pavement without speaking; then Guido said: 'I'm going home now and when you come and see me I recommend you not to weep!'

'Tonight?'

'Tonight!'

That evening, before going out, Ginia did a special toilette in Guido's honour. She felt her legs give way as she thought of him. She went up the stairs in a state of panic. She listened at his door; there was a light but no sound of conversation. Then she coughed as she had on a previous occasion but nothing stirred within. She decided to knock.

Fifteen

Guido, smiling, opened it, and a girl's voice from the back of the room called out, 'Who is it?' Guido offered his hand and asked her to come in.

In the half-light by the curtain a girl was slipping on her mackintosh. She had no hat, and she looked Ginia up and down as if she owned the place.

'A colleague of mine', said Guido. 'It's only Ginia'.

The girl went to the window, biting her lips and inspecting herself in the dirty glass. She had the same kind of walk as Amelia. Ginia looked first at her and then at Guido.

'Well, Ginia?' said Guido.

The girl finally left but not before looking her up and down for a last time from the door. She slammed it and they heard her footsteps gradually die away.

'She's a model', said Guido.

That night they stayed on the sofa with the lamp lit, and Ginia no longer made any attempt to hide away. They had moved the stove up to the sofa edge, but it was still cold, and after Guido had looked at her for a moment, Ginia went back under the blanket. What thrilled her most as she lay stretched out beside him was that this was real love. Guido got up, still undressed, to get a drink and hopped back quickly out of the cold. They placed their glasses on the stove to warm them. Guido smelt of wine but Ginia preferred the warm smell of his flesh. His chest was covered with curly hairs which brushed against her cheeks, and when they threw back the covers, Ginia compared her skin with his and was abashed and contented at the same time. She whispered in his ear that looking at him made her feel shy and Guido replied that she did not need to look.

Only when they were locked in an embrace did they finally say anything about Amelia, and Ginia told him that a woman was responsible for it all. 'She's brought it on herself', said Guido. 'You can't fool around with these things'.

'How you smell of wine', said Ginia in a low voice. 'It's better than the smell of bed', retorted Guido, but Ginia stopped his mouth with her hand.

They then put the light out and lay quietly. Ginia stared up at the ceiling in a vague way and thought of so many things, while Guido lay breathing heavily at her side. Distant lights could be seen over by the windows. The smell of wine and warm breath conjured up Guido's landscapes. Then she wondered if her frail body was to Guido's liking and whether he would not prefer the slender, dark and handsome Amelia. Guido kissed her all over in silence.

Then she became conscious that Guido was asleep and felt they could not go sleeping like this, locked in each other's arms, and she disengaged herself gently and found a cool spot, then she felt uncomfortable, naked and alone. Again she was overcome with a kind of nausea, as when they bathed her as a child. She wondered why Guido made love to her and thought of the next day and all the days she had waited for, and her eyes filled with tears, and she wept quietly to herself so that no one could hear.

They got dressed in the dark and Ginia suddenly asked who the model had been.

'Just a poor devil who had learned of my return'.

'She's good-looking, isn't she?' said Ginia.

'You saw her, didn't you!'

'But how can people pose in this cold?'

'You girls don't feel it', said Guido, 'you are made to be naked'.

'I couldn't do it'.

'But you have tonight!'

Guido looked at her; she could see him smiling. 'Happy?' he said. They sat side by side on the sofa and Ginia rested her head on his shoulder so as to avoid looking him in the eyes. 'I am so afraid that you don't love me', she said.

Then they made some tea, and Guido sat and smoked a cigarette while she strolled round the room. 'It seems to me I let you do what you like. I have even sent Rodrigues out for a walk the whole evening'.

'Will he be back any moment now?' asked Ginia.

'He hasn't the door-key. I am going to take it down'.

They parted at the door therefore because Ginia wanted to avoid seeing Rodrigues. She went back in the tram, feeling gloomy and without thinking about anything in particular.

She had embarked on her real life as a lover because she and Guido had now seen each other naked and everything seemed different. She felt as if they were married; even when she was alone, she had only to recall the expression in his eyes and her loneliness vanished. 'Is this what being married is?' Had her mother been like this? She could not believe other people in the world had ever had the necessary courage. No woman, no girl, could have seen a naked man as she had seen Guido. Such a thing could not happen twice.

But Ginia was not a fool and knew that all of them said that. Even Rosa that time when she wanted to commit suicide. The only difference was that Rosa did her love-making in the fields and did not know the joy of chatting and being with Guido. Yet even in the fields it had been nice with Guido. Ginia's thoughts kept returning to those times. She cursed the snow and the cold weather which stopped them doing anything, and thought, numb with anticipation, of next summer when they would all go to the hills, have walks at night and have their windows wide open. Guido had said, 'You ought to see me in the country. It is the only place where I can paint. No woman is as beautiful as a hill'. Ginia was happy because Guido had not taken the model on and intended, instead, to make a picture which was to extend all round a room as if the wall was open and they would see hills and blue sky on every side. He had been working it out while he was in the army and now he messed about all day with strips of paper; he daubed them with his brush, but they were only try-outs. One day he said to Ginia. 'I don't know you well enough to do your portrait. Let us wait for a bit'.

Rodrigues was hardly ever to be seen. By the time Ginia came to the studio before supper, he had already gone out to the café. Others came instead to spend the evening with Guido – including women, because Ginia on one occasion saw a cigarette-end smeared with lipstick – then it was that in order to please him – she said she was afraid she was disturbing him, these people made her feel nervous. She suggested to Guido he should leave the door open when he was on his own and wished to see her. 'I would always come, Guido', she said. 'But I realize that you have your own life. I don't want you ever to find me a bore when we are alone'. Saying things like that gave Ginia acute pleasure, comparable to the pleasure of being locked in his arms.

All the same, the first time she found the door closed, she was unable to resist the impulse to knock, feeling very tense.

Amelia sometimes came to her house after supper, wearing a worried look and her eyes sunken. They would go out immediately, for Ginia did not want her sitting on the bed, and they walked round the town until three o'clock in the morning. In her devil-may-care way Amelia would enter a bar and take a coffee, leaving traces of lipstick on the side of the cup. When Ginia told her that she might infect the cups, she replied. 'They wash them, don't they', shrugging her shoulders. 'After all, the world is full of people like me. The only difference is that they don't know'.

'But you're a lot better', said Ginia, 'your voice is not so husky'.

'Do you think so?' replied Amelia.

They did not pursue the matter further and Ginia, who had so many things to ask her, did not dare. The only time she alluded to Rodrigues, Amelia looked black and said, 'Take no notice of those two'.

But one evening she arrived at the house and asked her, 'Are you going to Guido's tonight?'

'I don't know', said Ginia, 'he may have company'.

'And are you going to let him get into this bad habit of not being disturbed? You stupid fool, if you're as humble as this, you'll never get anywhere'.

Ginia told her as they were on the way there that she thought she must have quarrelled with Rodrigues.

'He's as big a swine as ever', said Amelia. 'Did he say that? And to think that I saved his skin for him!'

'No. He merely said that it is all an excuse you have faked up for making love with that doctor chap'.

Amelia began to laugh grimly. When they had got as far as the studio porch, Ginia saw a light in the window above and felt desperate because up to that moment she had been praying that Guido might be out. 'There's no one there', she said. 'Don't let's go up'. But Amelia resolutely entered.

They found Guido and Rodrigues lighting the fire in the hearth. Amelia went in first, followed by Ginia, forcing a smile. 'Well, look who is here!' said Guido.

Sixteen

Ginia asked if they were disturbing them and Guido darted an odd look which she could not interpret. Near the fire-place was a stack of wood. Amelia had gone over to the sofa and sat down, remarking quietly that it was cold. 'It depends on your circulation', shouted Rodrigues from by the fire-place.

Ginia wondered whoever could be coming that evening, seeing they had even lit the fire. The wood had not been there the day before. No one spoke for a moment and she was ashamed of Amelia's offensive remark. When the wood had properly caught, Guido said to Rodrigues, without turning round, 'Keep blowing'. Amelia broke into a comic laugh and even Rodrigues' face lit up with pleasure. Then Guido got up and put out the light. The room, now filled with dancing shadows, looked quite different.

'We're always the same together, we lot', said Amelia from the sofa. 'How cosy it is'.

'We only need some roast chestnuts', said Guido. 'The wine's here'.

Then Ginia removed her hat, contented, and announced that the old woman at the corner sold roast chestnuts.

'It's Rodrigues' turn', said Amelia.

But Ginia quickly ran downstairs, only too pleased that they were not offended any more. She had to wander around for a while in the cold because the old woman was not there, and as she did so, she reflected that Amelia would not do what she was doing for anybody. She got back tired out. Among the darting shadows she could make out the figure of Rodrigues curled up back there by the sofa at Amelia's feet, Amelia was lying back;

it was just as it had been on that other occasion. Guido was standing up, smoking and chatting away in the red glow.

They had already replenished their glasses and they were discussing pictures. Guido spoke of the hillside he wanted to paint: his idea was to treat the subject as if it was a woman lying extended with her breasts in the sun and he was going to give it the flavour and taste of women. Rodrigues said, 'It's been done before. Change it. It's been done'.

They went on to discuss whether in point of fact such a picture had been done before, at the same time eating their chestnuts and throwing the shells into the fire. Amelia threw hers on the floor. Then Guido held forth: 'But no one has ever combined the two; I am going to take my woman and stretch her on the ground as if she was a hill against a neutral sky'.

'A symbolic picture then. Paint the woman in that case without the hill', snapped Rodrigues.

Ginia had not gathered it at first, but it turned out that Amelia had offered to sit for Guido, and Guido had not refused.

'What, in this cold weather?' asked Ginia.

They ignored her remark, and proceeded to discuss where the sofa should be placed so as to get both the daylight and the heat from the fire.

'But Amelia is ill', said Ginia.

'And what's wrong with me?' flashed Amelia. 'My work won't involve moving around'.

'It will be a moral picture', said Rodrigues, 'it will be the most moral picture there ever was!'

They laughed and joked about it, and Amelia, who had refused all drinks so far, as a precaution, now asked for one and said it would be safe if the glass was rinsed out with soap and water. She said that was what they did at home, and described to Guido the treatment she was getting from the doctor and joked about the injections. She told him he need have no anxiety because her skin was quite healthy now. Ginia spitefully asked her if her breast was still inflamed. Amelia flew into a rage and retorted that she had got better breasts than hers. Guido chimed in, 'Let's see!' They all exchanged glances and laughed. Amelia unbuttoned her blouse and loosened her brassière and displayed her breasts, supporting them in her hands. They had put the light on. Ginia looked quickly across but she could not face the malicious triumph that shone in Amelia's eyes.

'Now let's see yours', said Rodrigues.

But Ginia shook her head. She was suffering agonies. She looked on the ground to avoid Guido's gaze. Some seconds passed and Guido said nothing.

'Come on!' said Rodrigues. 'Let's drink a toast to yours!'

Guido was still silent. Ginia suddenly turned towards the hearth, feeling that they thought her a fool.

So next day Ginia went to the shop, knowing that Amelia, in the nude, was alone with Guido. There were moments when she felt she was dying. She had a picture of Guido's face staring at Amelia continually before her. She could only pray that Rodrigues was also present.

During the afternoon she managed to get away on the pretext of delivering a bill. She ran to the studio and found the door locked. She listened; there was no one there, apparently. Then she went downstairs in a calmer frame of mind.

At seven in the evening she found them all at the café. Guido was wearing the famous tie and was smartly dressed. Amelia was smoking as she listened. They asked Ginia to sit down as if it was a child they were addressing. They talked of old times and Amelia talked about her artist friends.

'And what are *you* going to tell us?' whispered Rodrigues.

Without even turning her head, Ginia said, 'I'm a good girl'.

They then went down to the arcades to stroll around for a while, and she asked Guido if they could meet after supper.

'Rodrigues will be there', said Guido. Ginia gave him a

despairing look, and they arranged to meet outside for a few minutes.

It was snowing that night; Guido suggested going to the café for a glass of punch, which they drank at the counter. Ginia, shivering with cold, asked him how Amelia could bear to sit for him in such cold weather. 'It is warm by the fireside', said Guido, 'and she's used to it'.

'I couldn't stand it', said Ginia.

'And who asked you to?'

'Oh, Guido', said Ginia, 'why do you talk to me like this? I only mentioned it because Amelia is ill'.

Then they went out and Guido took her arm. They had snow on their mouths, eyes, everywhere. 'Listen', said Guido, 'I know all about it. I know you go in for these things too. There's no harm in it. All girls seem to like kissing each other. Live and let live'.

'But Rodrigues . . .' Ginia began.

'No, you are all as bad as each other. If Rodrigues is the one you want to sit for, go ahead, come tomorrow. I don't expect you to account for everything you do in the day'.

'But I've no desire to pose for Rodrigues'.

They parted company under the porch and Ginia returned home in the snow, envying the blind who beg for alms and have ceased worrying themselves about anything.

Next day at ten o'clock she dashed into the studio. She informed Guido at the door that she had chucked her job.

'It's only Ginia', Guido shouted back into the room.

Snow could be seen on the roof-tops. Amelia was sitting on the couch in the nude. It had been placed lengthways before the lighted fire. She contracted her shoulders and implored her to shut the door.

'So you thought you'd come and keep an eye on us', said Guido, turning towards the easel. 'Of which one of us are you jealous?'

Ginia sulkily approached the fire. She did not look at Amelia nor move over to Guido. Guido threw some more wood on the fire, which made the place hot enough for anyone to pose in the nude. As she went by, he slapped her playfully on the back of her neck with his open palm, and while Ginia was turning her head, he stroked Amelia's knee as if he were touching a flame. Amelia, who was lying on her back, rolled over to turn her hip towards the heat, waited until Guido had gone back to the window, then whispered huskily, 'Have you come to see me?' 'Has Rodrigues gone out?' Ginia asked in reply.

Guido shouted instructions from the window. 'Raise your knee a little!'

Then Ginia plucked up the courage to turn round and looked at Amelia enviously as she moved away because of the intense heat. Guido, from where he stood at the easel, darted a rapid glance at both of them, which he immediately transferred to his sheet of paper.

Finally he said, 'Get dressed, I've finished'. Amelia sat up, pulling her coat over her shoulders. 'Done!' she laughed. Ginia sidled up to the easel. Guido had drawn an outline of Amelia's body on a long strip of paper. Some of the lines were simple, others intricate. It was as if Amelia had become fluid and flowed on to the paper.

'Do you like it?' said Guido. Ginia nodded as she tried to recognize Amelia. Guido laughed at her.

Then Ginia, her heart beating fast, said, 'Draw me too!'

Guido raised his eyes, 'Would you like to pose?' he said. 'In the nude?'

Ginia looked over in the direction of Amelia and said, 'Yes'.

'Did you hear that? Ginia wants to pose in the nude', shouted Guido.

Amelia laughed by way of reply. She started up and ran off towards the curtain, wrapping her coat round her as she went.

'You undress there, by the fire, I'm getting dressed here'.

Ginia gave a last look at the snow on the roofs and murmured, 'Shall I really?'

'Go ahead!' said Guido. 'We are not strangers'.

Ginia undressed near the fire, slowly but with her heart thumping so hard that she was shaking all over, and blessed Amelia for going off to dress elsewhere, so that she would not be looking at her. Guido snatched the sheet of paper off his board and pinned up another. Ginia put her things down on the sofa one by one. Guido came up and poked the fire. 'Hurry', he said, 'or I'll be using up too many logs!'

'Courage!' shouted Amelia from behind the curtain.

When Ginia was naked, Guido examined her slowly with his clear eyes. His expression was serious. He took her hand and flung a portion of the rug on to the floor. 'Stand on that and look towards the fire', he instructed, 'I am going to do you standing'.

Ginia stared into the flames, wondering if Amelia had already gone out. She noticed that the heat was making her skin red and was scorching her. Now she could see the snow on the roofs without craning her neck round.

'Don't cover yourself with your hands. Raise them as if they were reaching up to a balcony', came Guido's voice.

Seventeen

Ginia stared smiling into the fire. A shudder ran through her. She heard Amelia's light tread and saw her appear by Guido's side near the window: she was adjusting her belt. He smiled at her without turning round.

But she could hear another step close to the sofa. She was on the point of lowering her arms.

'Keep a natural pose', said Guido.

'How pale you are', remarked Amelia, 'forget about us!'

At that moment Ginia grasped what was happening and was so frightened that she could not even turn round. Rodrigues had been there all the time behind the curtain and he was now in the middle of the room, looking at her. She imagined she could even feel his breath. She went on staring into the fire, and, like a fool, trembled all over. But she could not turn round.

There was a long pause. Guido was the only one who stirred. 'I am cold', she whispered inaudibly.

'Turn round, take the jacket and chuck it over yourself', Guido said at length.

'Poor thing', said Amelia.

Ginia now turned round quickly and saw Rodrigues standing open-mouthed. She picked up her things and covered herself. Rodrigues with one knee bent forward on the couch, gasped like a fish, and smirked. 'Not bad', he said in his normal voice.

While they were all laughing and trying to cheer her up, she ran barefoot to the curtain and desperately flung on her clothes. Nobody followed her. Ginia tore the waistband of her knickers in her hurry. Then she stood there in the semi-darkness; the sheets of the unmade bed nauseated her. They were all quiet outside.

'Ginia', said Amelia near the curtain, 'may I come in?' Ginia clutched hold of the curtain and did not reply.

'Leave her alone', said Guido's voice, 'she's a fool'.

Ginia began to weep silently, clinging to the curtain. She wept bitterly as she had that night when Guido slept. It seemed to her that she had never done anything else with Guido but weep. At intervals she stopped and said, 'Why don't they go away?' She had left her shoes and stockings by the sofa.

She had been weeping some time and felt quite numb, when the curtain suddenly opened and Rodrigues handed her her shoes. Ginia took them without a word and only half saw his face and the studio behind him. She then realized how foolishly she had behaved, to be frightened like that. The others were no longer laughing now. She noticed that Rodrigues had stopped still in front of the curtain.

She suddenly was afraid that Guido would come and ridicule her unmercifully. She thought, 'Guido is a peasant; he will treat me badly. What crime have I committed by not joining in the laughter'. She slipped on her shoes and stockings.

She came out without looking at Rodrigues or any of them. She just saw Guido's head behind the easel and the snow on the roofs. Amelia rose from the couch, smiling. Ginia snatched up her coat from it, took her hat in her free hand, opened the door and ran out.

When she was alone in the snow, she still felt naked. All the streets were deserted; she did not know where to go. However little they had wanted her up there, they had not been surprised to see her at that hour. She found distraction in the thought that the summer she had hoped for would now never come, because she was alone and would never speak to anyone again; she would work all day and Signora Bice would be satisfied. It suddenly occurred to her that Rodrigues was not really to blame; he always slept on until midday and the others had woken him up; it was not surprising that he had looked. 'If I had a figure like Amelia's, I would have taken them all aback. Instead of which I wept'. Her tears returned at the mere recollection.

But Ginia could not despair utterly. She knew she had been foolish. All the morning she contemplated suicide, or thought that at least she had caught pneumonia. It would be their fault; they would be sorry later. But it was not worth committing suicide. She had wanted to behave like a fully grown woman and it had not come off. It would be like doing away with yourself for having dared to set foot in a luxury establishment. When one is a fool, one goes home. 'I am just a poor girl in disgrace', she said to herself, walking close to the wall.

She felt cheered up that afternoon when Signora Bice called out as soon as she set eyes on her, 'But what a life you young girls lead. You've got the look on your face like somebody who's going to have a baby'. She told her that she had felt feverish that morning, glad at any rate that her suffering had been noticed. Returning home, however, she powdered herself up a bit on the stairs; she would feel ashamed in front of Severino.

That evening she sat waiting for Rosa, for Amelia, and finally for Rodrigues; she had decided to bang the door in the face of whoever called. No one came. In order to tease her, Severino threw a pair of socks full of holes on to the table, asking her if she wanted him to go about barefoot. 'Whoever marries you will be in a fine mess', he said to her. 'If mamma was here you would see'. Ginia, smiling, her eyes still red with tears, replied that she would sooner die than get married. That evening she did not wash up. She stood at the door, waiting instead. Then she passed through into the kitchen, avoiding the windows so as not to see the roofs white with snow. She came across some cigarettes in one of Severino's pockets and began to smoke one. She saw she could now cope with it; then she flung herself down on the couch, breathing hard almost as if she was ill, and decided she would smoke again tomorrow.

The relief Ginia felt at present because she no longer had to

99

run round doing things infuriated her because she had learnt to do everything at high speed and she now had so much leisure on her hands in which to think. Smoking was not much help; her chief concern had been to be seen in the act and now not even Rosa came to look her out.

The worst time was the evening when Severino went out and Ginia waited on and on, always hoping one of the crowd would turn up and yet unable to bring herself to go out. On one occasion a shudder ran through her like a caress as she undressed to go to bed; she stood before the mirror and looked at herself confidently, raised her arms above her head and slowly pivoted round, her heart beating fast. 'Supposing Guido should come in now, what would he say?' she wondered, knowing very well that Guido no longer gave her a thought. 'We did not even say goodbye to each other', she murmured and dashed into bed so as not to burst out crying in her naked state.

Sometimes Ginia would stop in the streets as she suddenly became aware of the smells of summer, its sounds and colours and the shadows of the plane-trees. She thought of them while she was still surrounded by mud and snow; she would stop at the street-corners, desire catching at her throat. 'It *must* come, the seasons never change', but it somehow seemed improbable now that she was all alone. 'I'm an old woman, that's what it is. All the good days are over'.

One evening when she was hurrying home, she met Amelia by her porch. It was a hasty meeting; they did not bother to greet each other properly, but Ginia stood still. Amelia with her veil was walking up and down expectantly.

'What are you doing?' 'I am waiting for Rosa', said Amelia in a husky voice, and they looked at each other. Then Ginia frowned and dashed upstairs.

'What's the matter with you tonight?' asked Severino between mouthfuls. 'Have they given you the go-by?'

When she was alone, Ginia began to fall into real despair.

She was past tears. She paced round the room like one possessed. Then she flung herself on the sofa.

However, Amelia turned up later that evening. At first, as she opened the door, she could hardly believe it. But Amelia entered as if nothing was different and asked if Severino was in; then she sat down on the couch.

Ginia forgot all about smoking. They discussed what they were doing, really for something to say. Amelia threw her hat down and was sitting with her legs crossed; Ginia was leaning against the table by the lamp, which was turned low, and could not see her face. They talked about the terrible cold, and Amelia said, 'I've had my share of it this morning'.

'Are you still undergoing treatment?' asked Ginia.

'Why, do I look different?'

'I don't really know', said Ginia.

Amelia asked if she could have a cigarette there was a packet on the table. 'I smoke now, too', said Ginia.

While they were lighting up, Amelia said, 'Is it all over then?'

Then Ginia blushed and did not reply. Amelia looked at her. 'I thought as much', she remarked.

'Have you just been there?' stammered Ginia.

'What does it matter?' said Amelia, uncrossing her legs and jerking on to her feet. 'What about going to the pictures?'

As they were finishing their cigarettes, Amelia laughed and said, 'I have had a bit of luck with Rodrigues. He wanted to know if I loved him. Now Guido is jealous'. And while Ginia forced a smile, she went on, 'I am very bucked – I am going to be cured by spring. Your doctor friend said he took me in hand in time. Listen, Ginia, there's nothing particularly good on at the cinema'.

'We can go where you like', said Ginia, 'you lead the way'.

PENGUIN EUROPEAN WRITERS

DEATH IN SPRING
by Mercè Rodoreda
With an introduction by Colm Tóibín

Death in Spring is a dark and dream-like tale of a teenage boy's coming of age in a remote town in the Catalan mountains; a town cut off from the outside world, where cruel customs are blindly followed, and attempts at rebellion swiftly crushed. When his father dies, he must navigate this oppressive society alone, and learn how to live in a place of crippling conformity.

Often seen as an allegory for life under a dictatorship, *Death in Spring* is a bewitching and unsettling novel about power, exile, and the hope that comes from even the smallest gestures of independence.

'Rodoreda has bedazzled me' Gabriel Garcia Marquez

'Rodoreda's artistry is of the highest order' Diana Athill

'Read it for its beauty, for the way it will surprise and subvert your desires, and as a testament to the human spirit in the face of brutality and willful inhumanity' *NPR*

PENGUIN EUROPEAN WRITERS

THE LADY AND THE LITTLE FOX FUR
by Violette Leduc
With an introduction by Deborah Levy

An old woman lives alone in a tiny attic flat in Paris, counting out coffee beans every morning beneath the roar of the overhead metro. Starving, she spends her days walking around the city, each step a bid for recognition of her own existence. She rides crowded metro carriages to feel the warmth of other bodies, and watches the hot batter of pancakes drip from the hands of street-sellers.

One morning she awakes with an urgent need to taste an orange; but when she rummages in the bins she finds instead a discarded fox fur scarf. The little fox fur becomes the key to her salvation, the friend who changes her lonely existence into a playful world of her own invention.

The Lady and the Little Fox Fur is a stunning portrait of Paris, of the invisibility we all feel in a big city, and ultimately of the hope and triumph of a woman who reclaims her place in the world.

'A forceful affirmation of the human spirit' *Guardian*

'[Leduc] can capture the smells of a country childhood, dazzle with the lights of the Place de la Concorde or make you feel the silky slither of her eel-grey suit' *Observer*

'This book is as richly humane as anything else you're likely to read' *Independent*

PENGUIN EUROPEAN WRITERS

THE TRAIN WAS ON TIME
By Heinrich Boll

The hauntingly beautiful first novel by the winner of the Nobel Prize for Literature

Twenty-four-year-old Andreas, a disillusioned German soldier, is travelling on a troop train to the Eastern Front when he has an awful premonition that he will die in exactly five days. As he hurtles towards his death, he reflects on the chaos around him - the naïve soldiers, the painfully thin girl who pours his coffee, the ruined countryside - with sudden, heart-breaking poignancy. Arriving in Poland the night before he is certain he will die, he meets Olina, a beautiful prostitute, and together they attempt to escape his fate...

'His work reaches the highest level of creative originality and stylistic perfection' *Daily Telegraph*

'Boll combines a mammoth intelligence with a literary outlook that is masterful and unique' Joseph Heller, author of *Catch-22*

'My most-admired contemporary novelist' John Ashbery